PINNED FOR DEATH

BY

BEVERLY ANN MEYERS

D1714585

PINNED FOR DEATH

AKNOWLEDGEMENTS

This book is dedicated to my wonderful husband, Martin, who has assisted me and urged me on. His suggestions are greatly valued. He also was instrumental in creating the book cover.

My dear friends, Carol Levine, added her support and, Janet and John Silva, generously supplied the stickpin for the book cover.

The Wannabees, my extended family, have given me valuable suggestions and have offered great insight in order to make this book a success.

A LOVER'S LAMENT

Beware my love,
Beware my dear.
You walk the streets,
While death is near.

You stole my love,
Betrayed my heart.
You'll suffer the penalty
And I'll depart.

My revenge is nigh,
And I'll feed on your fear.
Beware my love,
Your death is near.

PINNED FOR DEATH

Chapter 1

Wednesday evening before Thanksgiving

The footsteps came closer. When she stopped, her pursuer stopped. As scared as Regina Costello was, the young woman needed to continue. The taxi stand was two blocks away. Only two blocks. Regina knew she could make it.

However, her condition held her back. Running wasn't an option. Regina stopped again because the flutter in her belly signaled the first time she felt life. The precious cargo carried in her womb stirred the maternal instinct to protect them whatever the cost. She picked up the pace. Could she get away? Be safe from harm? Less than two blocks now. Step by step …

A shadowy form caught up to her and forcefully spun her around.

"Oh, my God! It's you. What a relief." Catching her breath, "You scared me. W-why didn't you catch up to me earlier? We could've walked together to the taxi stand, and—"

"I've had enough. Enough of your treachery. I know all about it. You and your lover sneaking around behind my back."

Regina noticed the rage in the man's eyes. She looked up to him. "I-I'm sorry. How can I make it up to—"

A gloved hand reached out and pulled Regina close to him. A knife glistened in the dim light. The instrument came up and down in one thrust piercing Regina's chest. Her body stiffened. Her final thoughts were of her babies. She didn't have time to mourn their death.

Blackness enveloped Regina as she fell. Her inert form dropped to the cold pavement. For only a brief moment the person who lingered over the body felt remorse. Reaching into a coat pocket, the killer took out a small gold initial pin and secured it to Regina's coat lapel.

He grabbed the dead woman's left hand and tore off the glove in anger, savagely pulled off the engagement ring almost snapping the finger, and plopped the ring into a pocket. He removed the purse from the dead form, rummaged through it searching for any identification. A gloved hand found a credit card case and pocketed it. One deliberate toss threw the purse into the darkness.

Footfalls. Who could be coming? Rising and scurrying into the shadows the murderer crept close to the dark buildings with a sigh of relief.

The figure cloaked in darkness heard a young woman's voice.

Confident of complete safety, the killer continued and slithered to the end of the street and around the corner.

PINNED FOR DEATH

Chapter 2

Earlier in the day

The Frankford El's recorded voice announced, "Next stop Fifth Street Station for Independence Hall and the Liberty Bell. Fifth Street Station."

The El car's persistent jostling racked Regina Costello's body. Her stomach churned in continuous turmoil. She tried to quell the nausea by chewing some peppermint-flavored gum. The feeling made the trip unbearable. She needed to get off at 2nd Street, but the last lurch of the train as it pulled into Fifth Street Station changed her mind.

"Oh, God! I can't stand it. I must get off." She quickly stood, waves of queasiness attacked her. Regina felt the rush of enveloping sickness. Not meaning to push people aside, her abrupt movements only rewarded her with glares and soft curses. The attractive young blonde-haired woman made her way around bodies scrunched together.

Commuters were eager to enjoy the long Thanksgiving Day weekend with family and friends. Others were anxious to begin holiday shopping, or go partying, and Regina's forceful scrambling at the people, annoyed even the most complacent rider.

"Sorry." Regina apologized, as she tried to squeeze past a young couple while interrupting their amorous embrace. They shot looks of disdain barely

3

able to move to one side of the exit doors. The young boy raised his middle finger in Regina's face, but she ignored the gesture.

Finally free from the grip of the stifling heated car, Regina Costello was able to breathe and gulp down the feeling of nausea threatening to explode out of her throat.

If only I could have caught another cab. Oh, that's right! I'm such an idiot. Thanksgiving is tomorrow. With most people leaving work early, cabs are at a premium.

She checked her watch to see if she were running late. The exquisite mother-of-pearl dial showed her she had thirty minutes to spare. She could take her time to get from 5th and Market to 3rd and Chestnut arriving at La Mediterranean precisely at 6:30 p.m. Her belly only allowed her to climb the staircase from the El platform to street level a few steps at a time. All the carried items became heavier. A desperately needed rest to quell waves of nausea wasn't available.

La Mediterranean was her father's favorite continental restaurant. Old World cuisine, formal dining, housing antique décor. And Regina's favorite, too. She loved the red velvet draperies covering latticed windows spanning from floor to ceiling. Also the exquisite chandeliers graced intricately carved ceilings. Paintings of beautiful landscapes of the Southern European countryside hung on the walls.

PINNED FOR DEATH

There were some portraits, too. One in particular Regina especially adored: a young Italian farm girl with a wistful smile holding a basket of grapes draped down its side.

The restaurant celebrated for its generous portions of impeccably prepared food, and from its name, copied from fine Northern Italian, as well as traditional French cuisine. Joseph Costello, Regina's father, preferred the Italian offerings which always suited his discriminating palate. Wines decanted by finely-dressed servers wearing black tuxedos with crisp, white shirts and the inevitable black bowtie.

As she walked toward the restaurant, Regina thought about what she would discuss at her dinner meeting with her father. He asked to meet with her before the busy holiday weekend began.

She said to no one, while plodding toward the destination, "He's such a religious, righteous, pompous … But above all, and regardless of his faults, I still love him dearly and always will. Although he's been strict, he's been so good to me all these years."

Father, how can I disappoint you so? And I know that's what you'll think. I'm a disappointment. I'm pregnant and I will only be a disgrace to you.

"I must be careful how I explain myself to him. If he could only understand and stop regurgitating his Old World traditions."

Reaching the destination, Regina Costello's heart beat rapidly with trepidation. The bags containing the gifts were really weighing her down, but she managed to quicken her step as she walked toward the restaurant's entrance. She planned to tell him what had happened at the lawyer's office, her pregnancy, and, also, about the most sensitive of topics.

She dreaded defying him while she glanced down at the bulge her engagement ring made through her fine leather glove, as a sudden wave of nausea attacked her. The nauseous feeling didn't originate from her condition, it was due to the seriousness of what she needed to reveal to her father. She knew there would be no easy way to tell him and could only pray to find the courage.

Even with the resolve to tell him. What would he say to her? What would he do to her? Would she be cut out of his will? Would he deny her being his daughter? These questions nagged at her.

She sighed, "I'm here. I just hope this goes as well as I think it should." She took a deep breath and entered the restaurant.

Once inside, Regina smiled at the maitre d', who immediately recognized the lovely young woman. He embraced her, and they exchanged pleasantries. Not able to leave his station, the maitre d' whispered in her ear to tell her where Joseph Costello was seated waiting for her.

PINNED FOR DEATH

She put down the heavy bags, managed to get his attention, she waved briefly. He acknowledged her gesture with the nod of his head. She picked up her purchases and walked over to him.

"Ah, here you are, my dear. And you're on time, too. How wonderful," he said.

"Yes. Here I am." She bent to kiss her father's cheek.

"Here. Put those heavy things on this chair. That's right. Now. Let me look at you. Allow me to take in your beauty." His paternal eyes admired his daughter's loveliness. Her perfectly-shaped oval face reflected their family's ancestry. Costello mentally noted the slight bulge beneath her coat.

He smiled, "Why, you are absolutely glowing. Sit down, sit down. I've ordered a bottle of Chianti Classico, will you join me in some?"

"N-no, no. I can't. Really." Regina removed her gloves and coat and placed her things on an empty chair.

"Oh? Well, then you will have some of your favorite dishes I ordered for you, won't you? I know you are partial to French cuisine."

"Of course. I wouldn't want to disappoint you." Regina forced a smile, as she sat opposite her father.

He nodded to the waiter who began serving them. As they ate their meal, Costello started the conversation.

"Did you drive down, then?"

Flustered, she answered, "N-no. I-I mean, yes. Yes, I drove in to Center City. So I'd rather not have any wine."

Some time passed without conversation. Towards the end of the meal, he began, "So you're pregnant, then?"

"What?" Regina, taken aback, almost dropped her dessert spoon onto her lap.

"You can't hide it from me, my dear. I noticed it the moment you walked toward this table. You're pregnant, and it's why you're not joining me in this fabulous—" He picked up the wine bottle with a flourish and added, "How far along are you?"

"A-about five months," she admitted.

Her father leaned forward with disapproval in his voice. "I see. About five months. Pregnant. Oh, well, you don't know what you're missing. Now, tell me about your day." Costello poured himself another glass of wine then set the bottle on the table.

Regina sighed, "I went to see a lawyer about Marco's case."

"I see. And?"

"There is a chance. A rather slight one, though, the case can be reopened."

"Oh."

Regina stammered. "O-oh? Is that all you can say, is oh? I-I thought it's what you wanted. To have Marco's name cleared."

PINNED FOR DEATH

"Regina. It's what you wanted. What's done is done."

"What? Why? I can't believe I'm hearing this. I-I thought *you* are the one who wanted this done. I-I can't believe you're dismissing the opportunity of reopening Marco's case to exonerate him. Why?"

"Let's just say Marco isn't worth the trouble."

"What? He isn't worth the trouble? How can you, of all people, be so dismissive? All my life, it's been Marco this and Marco that. It's always been Marco. I've had to endure his insults, his taunting. And you. You always treated me as if I were second best. Always! I wanted to study abroad, but you squelched the idea with Mother. You convinced her I wasn't good enough to do anything but be your damn servant.

"But through it all, I've always loved you. I took it. I took everything. I was so stupid. And naïve. But no more, Father. No more. I live for myself. And for … and for—"about to blurt it out, but at the last minute couldn't bring herself to admit it. Instead, said, "my babies."

Joseph Costello rose from the table. "Regina! I am your father. Whatever I did for you was always in your best interests. I gave you everything. You're acting like a spoiled child."

"A spoiled child? Best interests? Sending me off to St. Agatha's, that-that prison of a girl's school was definitely not giving me everything. You don't know what I went through there with those stupid nuns."

"You are hysterical, my dear. Now, calm down. Think of the children you're carrying. You're causing quite a scene, you know."

"I could care less about causing a scene. I certainly will not calm down. I'm only getting started. I'm going through with reopening Marco's case, no matter what you say or think. He may have been nasty to me, but he's still my brother. And through everything he made me suffer, he deserves someone to care about his needs. If it's not you and Mother, it'll be me. I'll make sure he's cleared once and for all. I'm leaving."

"Wait. We can still talk this out."

"No, Father. Sorry I've caused you such displeasure. By the time my twin boys are born, I will be married so I'll be certain not to taint the family name," she declared with a sneer. "You'll be able to walk the streets of Society Hill with your head uplifted and unashamed."

"Twins? You're carrying twin bastard sons?"

"Yes. Sons. And they're *not* bastards, Father." She spat. "They are your grandchildren, for Heaven's sake. Will you never forget your old, out-dated … No, I suppose not."

"What about Eddie?"

"What about him?"

PINNED FOR DEATH

Joseph Costello's eyes glowered. "You're engaged to the man. Doesn't he have a say …"

"Consider the engagement broken. My being betrothed to him, your words, was strictly your idea. Not mine." Regina sniffed.

"Whose babies are they?"

"Certainly not his. I've been seeing Marco's friend."

"That Richard person?"

"His name is Richard Parker and we're in love. Madly in love."

The elder Costello banged his hand on the table. "I'll not have it! You'll marry whomever I tell you."

Regina's chair scraped the tile floor as she stood. "The hell I will."

"You're forgetting your bags."

"They are gifts for you and Mother. Enjoy them. Merry Christmas!"

Regina put on her coat, grabbed her purse and valise, turned on her heel, and left the restaurant.

As he sat down, Costello pulled his cell phone from its clip on his Spanish leather belt. The contact number was on speed dial. When the connection was made, he spoke into the device saying, "She just left. Yes, she did … And, yes, you're right. What she is proposing is a bit of a problem now. She's very angry and determined, you know … I agree … I think it's about time you cleaned up your mess … Well, do

11

whatever you think is necessary to make her listen to reason … Do you see her? … I see. You say she's passing you now? Good … Yes, and report back to me when you are finished speaking with her." He ended the connection. Snapped the phone closed, replacing the instrument on his belt. He relaxed satisfied.

***

Sometime later

The abrupt chirp from his cell awakened Joseph Costello from his reverie. Although he was expecting a call, he didn't think so much time had passed when he checked his watch. The cell's ID revealed who the expected caller was. He pressed the instrument to his ear as the person spoke of what transpired with Costello's belligerent daughter. As he listened, his amusement turned to anger when the familiar voice related the details of the events earlier in the evening.

In a harsh whisper, he spoke into the instrument. "You spoke with her? … And what was the outcome? … I know, I know. She may have sinned, but she is *figlia mia*! My daughter, do you hear? … And she refused to listen? … Then there is only one thing that must be done. I will speak with her and make her listen to reason … No, no you mustn't. This is my responsibility. I am her father." Costello snapped the phone closed and replaced it on his belt clip. He slapped down his napkin on the table, plunked several bills on the table, scooped up Regina's bulky packages and rose to leave the restaurant.

The maitre d' noted the Costello's hasty departure with concern and followed him. Catching up with the older man the maitre d' asked what the matter was.

Costello replied with much agitation, "This is a family matter which must be taken care of immediately." The maitre d' returned to his station remembering the man's remark and the look of absolute rage on his face.

Chapter 3

Engrossed in her own thoughts of her long working day, Alison Caldwell turned onto Ramstead Street, more like a narrow alleyway than an actual street, which she thought was a shortcut to the Frankford El. However, she made a terrible error in her haste to get home. Instead of turning left heading in the direction of the 8th Street station, she turned right toward City Hall.

She wrapped her arms around herself, trying to keep warm while striding to the El, as Alison spoke with excitement into the night at no one in particular, "I am so damn lucky to get a job as a paralegal at Dunbar, Engels and Quinn. Carlotta Ramirez is an absolute bitch to work with, but I'm learning so much from her. Sure she's tough. She's gotta be.

"Sorry, Keesh and all your good buddies. I wanted to party hearty, but ya gotta do whatcha ya gotta do. I'll make it up to you. Next time we go out, it'll be on me. Everything. Promise."

A little less euphoric, her stride slowed with each passing step.

Geeze! At night everything looks so different. Please, please don't let me get lost. "It's way after hours, I didn't realize how tired I am, and, all I wanna do is go home. Couldn't even party if I wanted to." She relied on her instincts to find her way to the train station, which caused her to almost trip over a crumpled form in the middle of the sidewalk.

Omigod! What's this? A street person deciding to take a snooze on the pavement? "Oh, come on, you. Get a damn job, will ya? I'm sick and tired of all you dumb asses begging for money. Get up, will ya? C'mon and get up and ... Omigod!"

Alison stopped speaking when she noticed the person's feet. A dull overhead streetlight's beam bounced off silver buttons on the side of the boots the still form was wearing. The legs were spread askew as if making a futile effort to run to somewhere but were, in fact, frozen in stride. One gloved hand was wrapped around something protruding from the chest.

"Omigod! Is that what I think it is? A knife? I nearly tripped over a murder?"

Cell phone. Alison pulled it from her shoulder bag. About to punch in the number one for 9-1-1, a squad car's siren pierced the night interrupted her. Alison turned her head in an abrupt about face and chased after the sound, trying to flag down the car traveling down 8th Street. She wasn't quick enough. The car went at a fast clip, and the stiletto heels of her boots didn't help much in the speed department.

Dejected, Alison made the emergency call. An operator answered immediately.

"Nine-one-one. What is your emergency?" The dispatcher asked in a detached tone.

"Uh, I'd like to, uh, report, a, uh, dead body."

"Male or female?"

"Uh, she's a female."

"And where is your location?"

"I'm at, uh, Ramstead Street, I think."

"Miss, are you sure or not?"

"Sorry. It's so dark on this street. The sign does say Ramstead."

"Are you sure?"

"Uh, yeah."

"Ramstead and where?"

"Uh, I'm not really sure. Like I said it's dark out here, and I can't read the other street sign. But I think I'm between 8th and 9th Streets. I guess."

"What's the condition of the body?"

"Condition? She's dead."

"I know that. Is this a joke? Because if it is, it's a felony and—"

"No, no, no! This is no joke. Look I'm out here alone with this dead woman in the street. And, and, you gotta get the police out here right now. Dammit. I'm not making this up. This is serious."

"All right. All right. Just calm down. I dispatched a squad car to your location ASAP. Stay where you are, okay? I'll need your name, miss, for the record."

"M-my name is Alison. Alison Caldwell."

"What? I didn't quite hear what you said. Again please."

PINNED FOR DEATH

"I said my name is Alli ... oh shit! This phone is about to poop out on me. Dammit! I'm Alison Cald ... well ..."

"I got it. Alison Caldwell. You calling from a cell?"

"Yes."

"I'll need the number to verify the info you gave me. Otherwise it'll take some time for help to arrive."

"Sure. It's 2-1-5-5-5-5-3-2-0-1."

"Say again? I only have the area code."

"It's 2-1-5-5-5-5-3-2-0-1—"

"Miss, mi ... ? Are ... still there? I c ... hear yo ... "

The phone went silent.

Thanks to the phone dying, Alison needed to wait until help arrived. The young paralegal bravely scrutinized the dead woman.

Her eyes had adapted to the dark so she could see the woman's body splayed in front of her. The long, blonde hair framing the face lay on the ground much like a layer of worms falling upon themselves trying to flee in all directions.

What stuck out in Alison's mind was the boots with the silver buttons on the side. Those boots she saw earlier in the day. The boots belonged to the young woman who visited Carlotta Ramirez' office.

It's Regina Costello. She wore those same exact boots.

17

The left hand, gloveless, was at the body's side.

Why is her left hand bare? Uh, oh. The ring is missing. She was robbed, then killed? Or, killed then robbed?

Fascinated Alison knelt beside the corpse. The eyes were open and staring at nothing. The knife sticking out of Regina's chest gave Alison pause. She was tempted to touch it, but didn't. Alison looked around to see if anyone was watching. There wasn't.

"You were supposed to be my heroine. I wanted to be like you. Who did this to you? Omigod! Is he still here?" she breathed. Alison was frozen in place not moving a muscle while checking the surroundings. The young girl tried to quiet her breathing in order to hear the faintest sound. Shuddering from fright and cold, Alison did a slow scan of the narrow street. Nothing was heard or seen out of the ordinary and she was able to breathe normally again.

Also, something was added.

"What's this? A pin on the lapel. Is this an initial pin like the one Regina showed us today? Can't see it too well in the dim light. Why would the killer put a pin on her coat? This is so absolutely weird."

Come on, come on, police guys. I'm like freezing out here. How long does it take for the police to come?

PINNED FOR DEATH

Alison rose and paced back and forth trying to keep warm. "I'm scared, but I guess I'm not supposed to leave her alone. Here *I* am alone with a dead cell phone and a corpse for company. What a night this has turned out to be."

It seemed as though hours had gone by, but when she checked her watch only five minutes had passed. Alison jumped when she heard slow, halting footsteps.

Chapter 4

Alison turned to see someone coming towards her. A tall, thin man wearing what appeared to be some sort of uniform: a long dark jacket with brass buttons down the front, dark baggy pants, and black boots. Most of his dark hair stuffed under a hat. Some loose strands of hair were blown back from his face by the ever-present wind. A scarf covered the right side of his face. The left side turned to the feeble light.

Relieved, Alison breathed, "Thank God you're here, sir. It seemed like I was waiting forever for someone to come. So I'm glad you're here."

"I know— " His voice trailed off.

Alison frowned at his comment. "You know? How did you know to come out here?" But then realized what he meant and added, "Oh, yeah. You must've heard me make the call to the dispatcher. How dumb of me."

The soldier was about to continue his thought, but instead his deep, gravelly whisper answered, "Yes, that's right. I heard you make the call." He looked down at her, sporting a crooked smile. "So here I am."

"Okay."

"I see you need some assistance."

Feeling perplexed, Alison started to say something, but lost her train of thought, when the stranger continued, "I was walking in this area. I

20

turned the corner and noticed you standing here. Don't worry, Miss. You're safe now. Come with me," he urged Alison, who took another quick look at the body on the ground. She turned back to him and stood on the sidewalk, deciding what to do next.

Still holding the dead cell in her hand, she looked at him again.

Something is bothering me about this guy. What is it? Just don't know.

He spoke well and seemed nice enough. She did feel safe knowing he was with her until the police arrived. Alison shrugged her shoulders when nothing seemed to click in her mind and replaced the instrument in the purse. But, then a thought came to mind.

"Uh, shouldn't we wait until the police come?" she asked warily. "At least, it's what happens on cop shows."

"Not a cop show. It's reality. Besides, this is a crime scene, and we should let the police do their job, don't you?"

"I know, but, I think we should wait."

"No. You might mess up the crime scene."

His explanation seemed logical enough. Yet something sinister lurked in the back of Alison's mind ready to strike out a warning like a cobra's hiss.

He walked closer to Alison in a slow, uneven gait.

BEVERLY ANN MEYERS

This situation is not right. I can almost smell it. He's not approaching Regina's body. Or even looking at her. He's not even curious? Why not? He's not telling me his name or showing me his ID. Wouldn't he?

"I'd rather wait, if you don't mind, sir," Alison said to the man trying to stall for time in order to think of something to do.

He's coming towards me. And he's scaring me. This is really bugging me.

"I-I mean leaving her doesn't seem quite right." With a nervous laugh, she added, "And, after all—"

Suddenly a squad car with blue-and-red flashing lights appeared from the opposite direction. Its shrill siren cut through the night making Alison turn to see bright headlights coming straight toward her, barely able to approach her in the narrow street. By pure instinct she shielded her eyes from the glare with one hand and waved at the car's approach with the other as the siren stopped. When she turned around, the man had disappeared.

Uh, oh! What's wrong with this picture? Why did he leave? If that guy was really just a passerby and wanted to help, why the hell did he leave? Uh, oh! He knows my name. I'm in deep shit. Real deep shit, and I don't know what to do about this, what if—

Two policemen rushed toward Alison.

"Are you the person who called about a body?"

"Uh, yeah."

"Are you all right, Miss?"

All she could do was shake her head from side to side. In a rapid-fire answer, she blurted out, "Nuh, uh. Nuh, uh. My, God. Something's weird. Totally badly weird. I was talking to a guy who I thought was helping me, and he left. I mean I turned around when I heard your siren, and when I turned back toward him, he disappeared." Alison gulped. "I was just talking to him when your patrol car showed up. And-and he's gone. Totally gone."

"Are you sure you saw someone?" The first officer asked.

"What?! Of course I did. What do you think?"

"Don't worry," the second one said more kindly as he touched Alison's arm. "We're Officers Michael Hedley and Frank Peterson. Frank, go see if anyone's around in this area."

"Sure thing." Peterson ran down the small street and turned a corner.

"Sorry. He's a rookie who's a bit overanxious about police work, and he's—"

"That's what's so weird. He didn't tell me his name. You told me who you both are. He didn't. Oh, God! I could've been taken to who knows where, if you guys, I-I mean, officers, uh, didn't show when you did. Oh, my God! Was he the murderer? He could've killed me too, and—"

"Are you okay?"

Alison looked up at Hedley and said, "I … don't … know … I … don't know …" Her voice wavered. She felt a bit lightheaded as the scene began whirling out of control. The detective instinctively caught her.

Hedley looked down at her while steadying her and asked, "Are you all right?"

"Yeah, guess so. Just a little dizzy, is all."

"Could you please tell me exactly what happened."

"Okay." Exhaling billowing clouds of vapor while trying to catch her breath, she began, "After I left my office, I took a shortcut to the El and went down this little side street when I s-saw her just lying there."

"That's the body?"

"Yep. That's her," she pointed at the corpse. "The body … right … there. I know who she is … She's, uh—"

More blinding lights appeared out of the darkness and two news vans practically plowed into each other as they attempted to enter the narrow street.

One was the Action 7 Newsvan with Linda Walters and Victor Oldman. They were followed by two cameramen in the other van. Oldman pushed his mike into Alison's face, as he asked her, "Is this where the homicide occurred?"

"Huh? Oh my God! It's you from the news and—" Alison exclaimed.

"Did you hear anything?" Oldman asked.

"Huh? N-no," she responded, a little disoriented.

"Do you remember anything else? See anyone?"

"I-I just remember her face all—" Alison answered automatically.

"What about her face?" Oldman asked.

"All right. All right," Hedley interrupted, putting up his hands to stop the interview. "That's all for now. This is a crime scene. Leave now. C'mon. You're interfering with the investigation." The news team grudgingly obeyed Hedley's orders and moved away.

Talking to Alison, "Okay, Miss. Come with me. Over here. Away from the body." To Peterson, he instructed, "Hey, Frank, guard the corpse, check it out, and make sure no one approaches it."

"Sure, Mike."

Hedley turned to Alison saying, "Miss, please come over here."

"What?" Alison asked.

"Listen. You can't talk with the press about what you saw. You need to tell me. Okay, now. What's with the face?"

"Oh, uh, okay, yeah. It's the first corpse I ever saw. Her face looked like a mask, is all." She wrinkled her brow.

Hedley continued, "Did you touch anything? Or did you do anything?"

"Oh, God, no! I know you're not supposed to. When I looked down at her, I saw her face staring back at me." Alison pointed with her chin into the street. She added, "I was so stunned at-at seeing someone lying in the street all messed up, you know, her clothes and all. It caught me off guard. I knew I needed to make a 9-1-1 and I did. I did what you're supposed to do. I thought I could give my phone a try because I forgot to charge it last night, and there was only a small percentage left. The dispatcher took all the info I gave her. But my cell quit on me when I was giving the dispatcher my cell's number."

Alison took a deep breath. Continuing, "She needed it to confirm my info. It's what she told me, you know. I don't know if she got it all. I-I guess she did, 'cause you're here. Then-then I saw this-this guy who walked toward me asking me questions, too. I thought he was a real nice guy, because he came almost right after I made the 9-1-1 call and tried to keep me calm and all. At first I thought that he was a policeman 'cause he came so fast after I made the 9-1-1 call. But I saw how he was dressed. Like a soldier. A-and he wanted me to come with him, a-and

I stalled going with him," Alison shook from the frightening events of the night.

"What did this man look like?" Hedley prompted.

"He wore a military jacket, you know, with the hat, coat with the brass buttons down the front and baggy pants. Let's see, very tall. About your height. And very thin. He spoke in a deep whisper. And, uh … his hair. Some of his hair hung down around his face. The wind blew it back, so I could see part of his face. Oh, and one other thing."

"What's that?"

"He had a scarf on. At least that's what it looked like to me. Almost like it didn't belong on his face."

Hedley replied, "A scarf?"

"Well, this, uh, scarf, or whatever it was, was draped across part of his face. Like he purposely covered it, ya know? It looked strange to me. The whole thing gave me the creeps. The more I think about it, the creepier it makes me feel."

"What color hair?"

"It looked black to me, I guess, but at least his hair was a dark color," Alison answered him. "Oh, God, sorry. I can't do this anymore. Can't I go, now?"

"Okay, okay. That's enough. It's been a nasty night for you. Why don't you take a breath," Hedley added, "It's a good thing you went with your instincts."

Peterson returned from scouting the immediate area and shrugged his shoulders at Hedley meaning the man was nowhere to be found. Peterson began inspecting the crime scene.

"Yeah," she breathed more easily speaking now. She looked straight up into Hedley's eyes. "Something wasn't right about him. You know?"

"Like what?"

"I can't put my finger on it. But his manner was … I don't know … very controlled and … uh, cautious. No, not cautious," she waved her hands in the air, trying to think of the correct word her mind was searching for, "he was uh, you know, persuasive. Yes, that's the word I was looking for. He was very persuasive. He could've lured me away. Do you think that's what happened to her?"

Hedley said, "Can't say for sure. It'll be part of the investigation. Do you feel better now?"

"Yeah, sort of, I guess."

Hedley asked, "Did you notice anything else?"

Alison replied, "No-o, it's so dark out here. Even with the street light, I couldn't see too much. He came around the corner and walked toward me."

"Do you remember anything else about this man?"

"No. I can't remember anything else." She hesitated for a moment, then continued. "Only what I've already told you."

PINNED FOR DEATH

Hedley made a mental note of what he observed. He asked, "Could you show me any ID? We need it for the report."

"Oh, yeah. Sure. I'm Alison Caldwell, and here's my driver's license," she said pulling the license from the front pocket of her purse. Her hand shook a bit, and she dropped the license on the ground.

Both Hedley and Alison almost bumped their heads together as each one bent down to retrieve the driver's license. Since Hedley was a bit faster, he quickly removed his glove and scooped up her license in his hand saying, "I have it, Ms. Caldwell." She mouthed a brief, "Thanks."

Hedley scribbled down Alison's information on his notepad he pulled from a pocket and handed back her driver's license. "You'll need to come down to the station to make a formal statement."

"Couldn't it be tomorrow? It's awfully late and all. I gave you all the info I could. Everything is so confusing with the reporters and all these cameras—"

"You aren't obligated to come with me, but it would be better if you did."

"Why?"

"Because you're a witness now. What happened tonight is fresh in your mind. If you wait, you might forget some important details, and that could hinder the investigation. You need to make a formal signed statement before you can go home, okay?" Hedley instructed.

"Really? Do I hafta?" Alison looked up into Hedley's eyes.

"Really. That's the best way to handle this. I'll make sure it doesn't take too long."

"Okay," she sighed. "Glad I knew not to go with the guy. But, I'm goin' with you, sir, 'cause I know you're the real deal."

"It's Hedley. Call me Officer Hedley. C'mon, Ms. Caldwell, let's go. Say, Frank, get the uniforms to cordon off this street with the barrier, make the call to forensics and can ya wait here 'til they arrive?"

"Sure, no problem. You two run along and I'll keep watch. I'll make sure the news people stay away from this street, and I'll be waitin' for the squad to show up."

PINNED FOR DEATH

Chapter 5

Alison reluctantly went with Officer Hedley to the Roundhouse. They walked in silence striding toward the squad car and got in. The night's horrible event consumed their minds as the squad car sped the few blocks toward Philadelphia's main police station.

Even though it was late at night, the station was buzzing with activity. Criminals were being processed and giving statements.

Officer Hedley led Alison to a small room. He opened the door for her and took her coat, placing it on the chair next to her.

"Now, Miss Caldwell. Would you like some coffee?"

"Uh, I'd like a hazelnut latte, please."

"Miss, this isn't Starbucks. A coffee with cream and sugar will have to do."

With a flick of her hand, "Oh, well, then, I'm fine, thanks anyway."

They both sat at a table.

"Please tell me everything you remember from the beginning."

"Okay. Well, I got up this morning, as usual, and ..."

Hedley laughed shaking his head, "No, I mean from when you saw the body."

"Oh, okay, but shouldn't I tell you how I know it's Regina Costello's body? I mean that would

31

help you quite a lot and get down to business to solve the crime, wouldn't it?"

Hedley's eyebrows arched. "You know who the dead woman is?"

"Yes, I was going to tell you, but I was interrupted by the news people."

"How do you know this?"

Alison looked the officer square in the eye. "Officer Hedley, I'm a girl, and I'm up on these things. It was the boots she was wearing. The neat boots with the silver buttons. When I first saw them on the dead woman's feet, the boots rang a bell. At first I thought she was a street person lying in the street, but when I noticed her feet, I remembered the woman who came to see Ms. Carlotta Ramirez was wearing the same, exact ones. I'm sure Regina Costello is the woman I found on Ramstead Street."

"Who's Ms. Carlotta Ramirez?"

"She's the lawyer I'm working with at Dunbar, Engels and Quinn."

"Oh. Are you positively certain about the boots?"

"Absolutely, positively one-hundred percent certain," Alison emphasized sternly.

"I see. Well, we'll have to see whether or not the medical examiner finds any ID on her. If none is found on the body, she'll still be considered a Jane Doe. It's nothing against what you're telling me, of course. It's procedure, is all. I'll make a note of it for my own report. Don't forget to include it in your statement. One other thing. How did you know the man you saw in the street was military?"

"Oh, well, you see, my brother did a tour of Afghanistan four years ago." Alison sniffed back tears. "He was driving a jeep on a deserted road when he ran over a land mine. He and three of his buddies were killed instantly. So I, uh, know what a soldier looks like."

"I'm sorry."

"Thanks. It's okay. I have a hard time dealing with it sometimes." Wiping away a tear which traced a watery line down her cheek, she continued, "My parents too. But, you know," she sighed, "you cope the best way you can."

Hedley decided not to press her about anything else and reached over to pat Alison's arm. "You've done well, Ms. Caldwell. Real well. Guess that's it for now."

"Okay. Still feel a little weirded out about this whole thing, but I'll be okay, I guess."

"Would you care for some water?"

"No, no, I'll be fine, thanks."

"Okay," Hedley smiled.

"Is that all? It seems as though something's missing. Maybe I should stay a bit longer to go over some other things in my mind."

"Yes, it would be very helpful, but aren't you anxious to get home?"

"I know but I want to help," she paused, then continued, "I know! I'll give you a brief summary of what happened today. Is that all right?"

"It would be more helpful if you write everything down."

"Oh. But, if I tell you what happened first, it would help me write things down in the right order. Here's what happened: the lawyer I'm working with, Carlotta Ramirez came to my desk asking for my help to work on reopening a murder case. The murder case was Regina Costello's brother, Marco. Marco Costello, who was convicted of murdering his fiancé, Jeannette Turner two years ago. Marco was sent to prison. He was involved in a fight there and now is in the prison hospital in a coma. But, Regina told us her brother, Marco, couldn't have done it. She swore up and down he was at an insurance convention at the time of the murder."

"I see, continue."

"Okay. Carlotta called me into her office to take notes so I could research the case to see whether or not it could be reopened. I had to go here to the Roundhouse for info on the case."

"Why couldn't you look the case up on your computer?"

"Oh, see, I've only been working at the firm for two months and I don't have access to old files. I have to be working there for at least ninety days.

34

Then I get my permanent ID card and the benefits, and all that."

"Oh."

Alison leaned closer to Hedley. "Well, anyway I had to go to the basement to do the research. I needed to go there and the place is really spooky. It felt like a tomb. I expected ghosts to appear at every corner of the place."

Hedley urged, "And?"

She noticed his impatience and continued, "Oh, sorry, this old fogey was at the information desk asking me for my ID so he could copy what I needed to research Marco's case. I gave it to him, but I forgot to take the call number of the case with me. He told me it was okay. He just needed the person's full name. The old guy looked so shriveled up. Doesn't anyone let him outside?"

The officer replied, "You mean Rupert Ott? He's very good at what he does. He doesn't bite."

"Yeah, but I was afraid he might do something else to me just as nasty. But anyway, he gave me the record of the trial and some other stuff I needed to look over so the info could be copied. And guess what I found?"

"What was it?"

"Jeannette Turner was murdered and her body was left in an alley... Ohmigod! Regina Costello was murdered just like Jeannette Turner. You know, with a knife in her chest. Then Marco didn't kill Jeannette Turner after all. He *was* framed like Regina said."

"Well, let's not jump to any conclusions. There's still a lot of investigating to do."

"Why not? Isn't it cut and dry? I mean the evidence is staring you right in the face that both murders are connected. There's a serial killer out there somewhere, and I could've been next. Am I next? I saw the person I thought was a soldier right after I found Regina's body—"

"Miss Caldwell, you can't assume it was Regina Costello who was murdered. It could be someone else."

"Really? And before I totally forget. There's something else you need to know."

"And, what is it?"

"Her ring was missing. Whoever did her took her ring."

"Ring?"

"Yeah, her big, beautiful diamond ring." Alison looked down and frowned. "I guess it was an engagement ring." She looked back at Hedley. "And the killer put a gold pin on her coat. I tried to see whether or not the pin had an initial on it, but the street was so dark I couldn't see."

"Why?"

"Because from what I read about the Jeannette Turner case, she had a pin on her lapel with the initial 'J'."

PINNED FOR DEATH

Hedley rested his hands on his chin. "You could've missed seeing the pin when Ms. Costello visited the office."

Alison insisted. "No. I'm very observant. If the pin was there, I certainly would've seen it." She looked straight into Hedley's eyes. "Jeannette Turner's body had a pin on it. So did Regina Costello. What do you have to say about *that*?"

"What you're telling me could be simply a coincidence."

"A coincidence?" Alison scrunched up her face. "You gotta be kidding. There's a connection between both victims and you're letting somebody get away with murder."

"Wait a minute." Hedley stood, briefly left the room returning with a pad and a pen. "I want you to write down your statement just as you told it to me. Don't leave anything out. I'll be right here if you need any help. When you finish, sign it and hand the statement back to me. This is police business now. You are to go home, enjoy the Thanksgiving holiday, and leave the investigating to the authorities. Okay?"

Alison picked up the pen and rolled her eyes toward heaven, she answered, "Yep. Tomorrow is certainly Thanksgiving."

He reached over to pat Alison's arm. "You've done well, Ms. Caldwell. Real well. Guess that's it for now."

After Alison finished writing the statement, the officer printed it, asked Alison to sign it. Hedley scanned the document into a computer. He gave her a copy. Afterwards, he offered to take Alison home.

"No, it's too far. I live in Frankford. If you could walk me to the El, it would be fine."

"Are you sure you'll be all right getting home? It is very late. The least I can do is give you a lift to the El."

"Yeah, another ride would be fine, thanks."

"Are you ready, Ms. Caldwell?"

"Yes," she said, much relieved. "I feel better now."

"Let's go, then," Hedley gave her another confident smile as he helped her on with her coat. He took her arm and led her out of the police station.

Chapter 6

When the headlights from the El reflected against the overhead beams, signaling its arrival, the train came to a smooth stop. The doors swished open, and the recorded voice announced 8th Street making all stops. Alison stepped inside the car, turned to bid the Officer Hedley good night with a broad smile and waved at him. He touched the top of his hat and nodded. The doors closed, and the train pulled out of the station.

She breathed a sigh of relief, and settled in her seat. There were only two other people in her car. One was a young woman fast asleep snoring with her mouth open. A slovenly male street person, reeking from stale urine, and rancid sweat, stood near the door. He passed gas while ogling her.

Just what I need now. An old fart erupting noxious fumes wanting to get into my pants and pockabook after what I've been through.

"I positively, absolutely pinkie swear I will never, EVER work late again." She declared staring at the poor excuse for a man.

She stuck her finger in her mouth while making gagging noises. Ancient Male Street Person backed away with a scowl knowing he wasn't going to score with Alison.

Alison slumped in her seat. *Ugh! The disgusting weirdos you meet on the El.*

***

In the next car behind Alison's, a lone figure shuffled over to the car door's window and observed her slouched in the seat. He was going to pass through the door, but stopped in his tracks when he noticed two people near the young girl. The man decided to stay where he was. There would always be another opportunity to do what he intended. He limped away, sat in a single seat and rode in silence.

PINNED FOR DEATH

Chapter 7

Later that night

Coroner Dominick Vitalli examined the young woman's corpse on the slab. Before he cut away her clothing, he scrutinized the body. He noticed short, dark strands of hair on the young woman's coat. He carefully pulled the hairs from the front of the garment with forceps and held them under his magnifier.

"Definitely not yours, my dear," he said to the young woman's corpse.

The coroner placed the hairs under the microscope and using its highest power, made a confirmation of his suspicions.

Human hair. Seven-point-five centimeters in length.

He inspected the individual hair shafts and found each dark hair was thicker than a normal hair should be. Vitalli discovered the hairs displayed a different color at the root which was gray.

"Ah, so the perp dyed his hair. An older man killing a much younger woman? Or, was he just prematurely gray? Won't know until the guy is caught, that is if it *is* a guy. Well, at least we have some evidence for a DNA test."

He dropped the hairs in a small plastic bag and labeled it. The woman's clothes were placed in a

41

larger plastic evidence bag. The forensics team had placed the knife in another evidence bag. The ME placed all of the evidence bags aside.

The naked form of the lifeless body stretched out before him gave him a feeling of déjà vu. Why did this particular case stir up old memories? Had it really been fifteen years since he was called to identify *her* body? His Marie?

Vitalli's mind raced back to the terrible night, when he was unavoidably detained at work. He attempted to race through two open murder cases he had been assigned at the last minute, trying desperately to finish his report on the autopsies. He wanted to hand in closed files so he could meet Marie for dinner. It would have been her birthday as well as their 20th wedding anniversary. Vitalli was determined to leave work at 5:30 p.m. to meet Marie at the Three Threes restaurant for their special rendezvous, their special day together.

He remembered the urgent phone call, interrupting his work. The body of a woman was found close to the restaurant. She was a victim of a drive-by shooting. Could he please come to ID the body. *Her body.*

When he arrived at the crime scene, Vitalli remembered touching her face, her hair, through gloved hands, careful not to destroy evidence. He stared at the cruel gaping hole between her eyes and looking into those eyes, which were once so pure, blue and once so full of life, had become dull, dark and muddy. He tried to make sense of what happened to his beautiful wife.

Vitalli could only look as another coroner was called in to whisk her body away. His eyes traced every move the medical examiner made, as his dear Marie was scooped up from where she lay only to be placed in a body bag, zipped up and taken to the morgue. The gut-wrenching siren's wail echoed in his brain, as the vehicle containing his wife's body declared the death knell of his life with her.

Why her? Why? Why?

He shrugged off the sensation and continued to inspect the corpse on the table before him. He caressed the blonde hair with soft strokes of the comb smoothing out the tangled mess into long tresses. He arranged the hair around the body's face while assessing the dead woman's features.

He mentally superimposed his late wife's face over those of the corpse. The facial features of both women were similar and yet different. There was a wider space between the corpse's eyes. The victim's mouth, now closed, curved into a definite bow as if waiting for a kiss.

When he was finished preparing the body, Dr. Dom Vitalli did a meticulous assessment of the chest wound. With forceps, he carefully prodded the tissue. Next he performed a y-cut with a circular saw to remove and examine the vital organs. Vitalli weighed each one and recorded his results.

Into the mike, he stated, "The victim, a Jane Doe, was brought in about 9:00 p.m. Age between the mid-twenties or early thirties in reasonably good physical shape. The abdomen is rounded and well developed displaying pregnancy. Will examine after physical report is complete. The chest wound is approximately 20.5 cm in depth and 5.0 cm in width. The weapon is a straight-edged knife. The skin surrounding the site is raised and jagged due to the removal of the weapon. Death due to a ruptured aorta. The heart was free of disease as was the other vital organs."

Vitalli turned off the mike and released his grip on it.

A voice called out. "Uh, Dom? Are you in here?"

"Huh? Bobby? What're you doing here in the dungeon so late? I didn't hear you come in."

"Oh, I've been here for a while. I'm just tyin' up some loose ends with the Foster case. Before I call it a night, do ya need any help?"

"Oh, yeah, I'd sure appreciate it. I'm over here working on the Jane Doe case picked up earlier. We have a tentative ID from a witness, but, as you know, she'll still be a Jane Doe until something definite comes in as to her identification. Come on back here for a minute, will you? I need some help turning the body I'm working on here."

"Uh, okay. Did you say a Jane Doe case?"

"Yes, you know about it?"

Bobby Pieri came towards the slab. "Just that it came in. *Paisan*, what can I do for ya? Who called this one in?"

"Don't know. You know, the usual. No ID on the body. We really won't know much of anything more until the police report from the crime scene comes in."

"Did you say a girl was brought in?"

"Yeah. Why?"

"Oh, dunno. Just curious, that's all." Pieri added, "Did the cops get a trace on the call?"

"Yes, Bobby. From what Trev told me, it's in the log."

Pieri stopped short and began sweating when he saw the woman's boot. The silver buttons glistened from the overhead brightness of the exam lamp. His eyes traced the corpse from the boot to her face. He was stunned. Pieri's stomach lurched. *Holy Jesus God! I don't believe what I'm seein'.*

Vitalli saw the reaction on Pieri's face and became concerned.

"Bobby, are you sure you're not coming down with something? You're sweating like a—"

Pieri interrupted, "N-no. I'll be all right. Give me a sec."

45

Vitalli sensed something was wrong. Pieri had been exposed to badly decomposed corpses without showing much emotion. In fact the lack of emotion from Pieri struck Vitalli as rather odd from a younger, inexperienced man. But as Pieri proved himself competent under the medical examiner's guidance, he became used to the younger man's detachment to human remains. Yet tonight, Pieri's reaction was quite out of the ordinary.

"Are you sure? I mean I could take a break from this and—" Dom's brow creased with concern.

"N-no. No. I'll be fine, honest."

"I know. She's so young. To see a young attractive person dead like that could be quite a shock. Take a breath."

Bobby Pieri did and seemed to recover his composure.

"Oh, jeeze, I knew I forgot something. This old brain is becoming more and more forgetful. Watch your step, Bobby. I forgot to put her other boot in the evidence bag," Vitalli warned. The older man removed the boot and placed it in the evidence bag.

"Help me turn her over, would you?"

"Oh, uh, sure," Pieri said in a hoarse whisper.

"Just be careful with this one. I need to see if there are any bruises on her back. As you can see, she was knifed, but she could've put up a fight. So there could be other injuries on her flip side."

PINNED FOR DEATH

Pieri complied with Vitalli's request and, with much trepidation, assisted the coroner as he slowly turned the body on its side. Vitalli inspected the back of the corpse. The older man poked here and there finding nothing unusual. Pieri, taking Vitalli's cue, helped the older man place the woman's body in its former position on the examination table.

Strange thoughts permeated through Bobby's brain as if blood leaked from an open wound as he stared at the corpse.

Her face is turnin' towards me.

It wasn't.

Her eyes are watchin' me.

They weren't.

Her mouth is gonna call out my name.

It didn't.

This is really freakin' me out. Pieri steadied himself against another exam table praying the woozy feeling would dissipate.

His nausea returned when he noticed something missing from the ring finger of the dead woman's left hand. The ring should have been there. What happened to it? Where was the diamond ring that once embraced her finger? Was it stolen? Who could have done this? Who could have taken it? Then a terrible thought invaded his mind: *he* did it. Pieri surmised her fiancé must have done it. She told him something to tick him off, and he did this terrible thing.

Pieri hadn't the nerve to ask about the evidence bag for fear of drawing attention to himself. For, why would he be so interested in a dead woman's effects? Wouldn't his interest be misconstrued? His involvement in the woman's demise? No, he must keep quiet. Hold his tongue. Avoid eye contact. Not let on to Vitalli or anyone for that matter, about his relationship with the victim.

But, his actions did, in fact, almost give himself away. The intense magnet drew him ever closer to the body. Her body. Bobby knew he needed to see the bastard who did this. Now. To find out what happened between them. Bobby considered what he was thinking could be a mistake. He wasn't sure. Maybe they had a fight and she was killed by accident.

Vitalli sighed. "There weren't any other wounds on the body. So, whoever is responsible, it was a quick strike. I wonder if she was attempting to run away, and the perp grabbed her to pull her back and stab. She probably didn't have time to react. Maybe surprised, at first, then began to struggle. Tried to breathe. This could've been a crime of opportunity. What do you think, Bobby?"

"Uh, I-I don't know."

"It looked as though she was reaching for the knife. You know, as if she were trying to pull it out. Any ideas?"

"Uh, gee, I just don't know, Dom."

48

"It's possible she even could've known her assailant."

"M-maybe, but I haven't any clues, here. Ya sure got your work cut out for ya."

"Thanks," Vitalli replied peering over his glasses at his assistant.

"Listen, I-I'd like to stick around to help ya out, but I gotta see someone."

"Right now? I thought you could stay for a while and see me finish this case up."

"N-no. I really gotta go. I need to see a guy I know about something."

"Oh, I see, you're leaving me here all alone. Boy, some assistant you turned out to be." Vitalli laughed.

"Uh, yeah, guess so."

"So, you're deserting me for somebody else? Sounds mysterious."

"Yeah, I guess. Sorry. It's somethin' that kinda came up all of a sudden."

"Nothing serious, I hope."

"No, Dom. Just something to straighten out," Pieri removed his gloves. He slapped them into the biohazards receptacle kept beside the examination table.

Changing the subject, Vitalli asked his assistant. "Bobby? When's she due again?"

"Huh?"

"Gina. When is her due date for giving birth? I know you told me before, but the old brain seems to be shorting out remembering dates if they're not written down."

"Oh, oh. Yeah. Sorry. Early March."

"Early March, is it?" *The last time I asked I could've sworn he told me Gina was due in June. Maybe I'm becoming more forgetful than I thought. Or maybe he told me wrong. Or, maybe ... Nah!* Vitalli brushed the troubling thought aside.

"I'm real happy for you guys. Glad to know your family's getting bigger. Maybe someday you'll meet someone to settle down with."

"Yeah. Thanks, Dom. I mean I haven't met anybody else since my girl was killed. But maybe someday—"

"You're still young, Bobby. You're only thirty-two. You never know. Say, Bobby, I never met Gina. When am I going to get the chance? Maybe sometime within the next few weeks we could make dinner a foursome. What do you say? You know Gina and her guy, and both of us?"

The color from Bobby's face drained for a minute but was quick to return to normal. He took a deep breath. "Sure Dom. I'll ask 'er. I-I'm sure she'd like that. Dom, I really gotta go now." Pieri made a hasty retreat.

"Whatever it is I hope it's not too serious, Bobby, while I'm here scratching my head over my date here. The only thing is, conversation in this case will be kind of dead," Vitalli returned to work and laughed at his own pun while waving off his assistant.

***

Taking a much-needed dinner break, Dominic Vitalli sat at the lab desk. He licked his fingers, one at a time, careful not to drip any excess olive oil or Cheese Whiz on the papers he was reviewing. He wiped his mouth and hands with a paper towel contemplating what transpired earlier in the evening.

Bobby acted so strangely. Why is this particular body keeping him on edge? If he knows who it is, wouldn't he tell me? These young people. Who knows what goes through their mind. Anyway, back to work.

Vitalli put on a new set of surgical gloves. He continued scrutinizing his findings on the corpse laid out before him. He removed the drape and picked up a pair of long, metal forceps to probe the woman's body.

"Let's find out if there are any secrets you're keeping."

Vitalli felt around the abdomen just below the navel. He nodded as he felt the full roundedness of the belly. He put aside the forceps, took a scalpel from the tray, and proceeded to make a long, horizontal cut above the pubic hair, as if he were about to perform a cesarean section. He gently pulled the skin up and over the upper abdomen. He made another horizontal cut through the outer uterine wall and discovered exactly what he suspected ... two fetuses.

God in Heaven! Is this Gina's body? What will Bobby do if this is Gina? Is it why he was acting so strangely? Is he somehow involved?

The terrible thoughts racked his brain. Was the evidence he found a terrible coincidence? But his findings showed she carried twins. How much of a coincidence was *that*?

Vitalli placed the victim's hand on a glass slide pressing each finger down. Next, he put the slide in a baggie and labeled it. He reached for the labeled bag with the hairs from the dead woman's coat and placed both bags in a larger one for a comparison DNA test.

Vitalli sighed and shook his head as he meticulously injected a sterile needle into the delicate embryonic sacs extracting the amniotic fluid. He squirted the syringe's contents into another test tube, labeled it and dropped it into the bag with the other two items.

Next, he filled in the form requesting a DNA test to have on file. He reached up above his head and pulled the mike close. He spoke into the instrument to conclude his findings.

"Addendum to autopsy report on Jane Doe, homicide victim number 382, as of 25 November.

PINNED FOR DEATH

Vitalli exhaled as he recorded his final entry. "From examination of the lower abdomen, a horizontal incision was made revealing the victim was in the second trimester of a dual pregnancy."

Chapter 8

Wednesday night coroner's lab 11:00 p.m.

"What have ya got for me on the Jane Doe, Dom?" Detective Trevor Jackson asked.

"Well, it's a simple case of a knifing. Cut and dry."

Jackson's eyes narrowed. "Very punny. Since when is stickin' a knife in someone so damn simple?"

Vitalli picked up a probe, held it like a cigar between his thumb and fingers while raising his fuzzy eyebrows up and down and bent over. "You think I know how these crazies think all the time? I just report my findings, Trev. You want to know what goes on between these maniacs' ears, go see a shrink."

Jackson snickered at Vitalli's good imitation of Groucho Marx.

"Sorry, didn't mean to make light of this case, but this is very disturbing, and I need some release."

"Don't sweat it. If ya weren't laughin' you'd be cryin'. What else did the autopsy show?"

"Well, she must've had quite a good night, until the attack, that is. Stomach contents showed she dined on escargot, pâté de foie gras, duck l'orange with sparkling water, and crème brûlée for dessert, I'm sure. And from the remains of her dinner, she was killed at least one hour after she ate the meal."

"Wow! Snails, duck, and what's the other stuff you said?"

"Pâté de foie gras?"

"Yeah, that. By the way, what is patay da foo goo?"

"Pâté de foie gras," Vitalli corrected. "Trev, you need to be introduced to some culture in your life. It's French for mashed goose liver. Very posh and very expensive. How about I treat you to a fancy dinner after this case is solved for old time's sake?"

"Uh, ick! If that shit's on the menu, I'll pass. Lemme think about it," Jackson gave a disgusted shake of his head. He crinkled his brow. "But anyway, thanks for the food lesson. So the guy treats her to some mash and a little bit of quackers with some bubble water to wash it all down. Then she certainly ain't no street girl."

"No, not this one. Well, you saw the way she was dressed. This is an upscale female we're dealing with here."

"If our vic was treated to this high-class food, how come he didn't top it off with champagne?"

"There's a good reason for it."

"C'mon, Dom, don't hold out on me."

"She was pregnant," informed Vitalli, "with twins no less."

"Preggers? Whew! How far gone?"

"Five months, I'd say."

"Jeeze! Didn't expect a multiple homicide. Any ideas about why she was killed?"

"Who knows? Maybe Miss Doe had an affair with someone. The baby's papa finds out, is extremely jealous, confronts her and kills her. I took some blood and did an amniocentesis. We could get lucky. Since we don't have a suspect, the only thing that could match is some hairs I found on her coat. I will have a record of her DNA and blood type within I'd say in about ten days."

"Any chance we can speed this up?"

"No. Ten days it is, as long as Jessie isn't backlogged in the lab, which she usually is this time of year."

"Well, then, we'll just hafta play the waitin' game."

"Yes, we will," Vitalli sighed.

"Dom, can ya be reasonably positive about the TOD?"

"Yes. I can give you a ballpark estimate. At least one hour after she ate would make her dying around 8:00 p.m., give or take a half hour on either side. From my findings there were no defensive wounds."

The detective came closer to the examination table.

"So ya still don't know for sure if it was a man or a woman who did her in, do ya?"

PINNED FOR DEATH

"No, Trev. The hairs I found were from someone who dyed their hair blue-black." Vitalli added, "So a man as the murderer is still in the offing."

Jackson offered, "I wouldn't rule out a woman."

The ME countered while raising his brows up and down again, "But, you know, these days some guys don't always act like guys, if you catch my drift."

Jackson snickered, "Yeah, I see where yer goin' with this."

Vitalli continued, "The perp had dyed black hair. As a matter of fact, the exact color is none other than, Clairol Nice N' Easy blue-black color #124."

"How can ya be so exact 'bout the hair color?"

"Each hair color has not only an exact color number, but a chemical signature. It's why the dyes are the same each time a batch is made. All the manufacturers do is follow the same recipe and voila! You got your favorite hair color. Every time."

"How do you know the hair was dyed?"

"I found gray tips at the end of each hair I examined."

"So from what you're tellin' me, the perp was in a bad need of a touch up. So's the killer coulda been an old coot?"

"Yes, that's what I'm thinking. To me, the murderer definitely has to be a man. Maybe the person who treated her to the classy meal. And I'm thinking she must've known her killer. Someone she had confidence in."

"Don'tcha think it could've been anybody she met on the street? Ya know, her bein' at the wrong place at the wrong time? Somethin' like that?"

"No. I really do think she knew her killer, and she was taken by surprise."

"Holy shit. The poor girl."

"Yes, it is a shame," Vitalli sighed. "Oh, damn. I forgot to place the pin in the evidence bag I found on the vic's coat."

"Did ya say pin? What kinda pin?"

Vitalli gave the detective a quizzical look. "Why? It's just a gold lapel stickpin people wear. I forgot to put it back."

Trevor Jackson stood there for a few seconds scratching his chin. "Is there a mark of some sort on it?"

Vitalli examined the item closely. "Yes. It's the initial 'R'. Could stand for her first or last name." To Jackson, "Are you all right?"

"Somethin's awful familiar about this Jane Doe case. When you mentioned the pin. I dunno. I guess when you're in the biz as long as I've been every case feels like the last one. But, *this* one. It has a familiar ring to it, ya know? This one reminds me of another case I was on a while back. It's where a young woman was killed in a back alley and stuffed in a dumpster. The vic had an initial pin on her lapel too similar to this one. Just can't remember the name of the other case. This is gonna bug the hell outta me to no end."

"Guess you have a point there. I feel that way, too, sometimes. All these cases coming in here," Vitalli made an open gesture with his hands.

"But anyway, are ya done with her?"

"Yes, I'm about finished here. I'll fax you my complete report as soon as I can. I want to review it, of course, to make certain I didn't leave anything out or miss something crucial. Is tomorrow morning, okay?"

"Well, don't forget, you're comin' to my place for Turkey Day. So do your thing ASAP and don't stay too damn late in this hole." Jackson shook an index finger at his friend. "Remember dinner's at five."

"Yes, I know. As always, thanks for having me."

"No prob. Oh, and when ya get a positive ID for the body, let me know so the family can be notified to make it official."

Vitalli answered with a wry smile as he peered at Jackson over his bifocals.

Jackson sighed, "Man, this case looks like it's gonna be a tough one ta crack. Guess I'll have some of the boys check around all the hip restaurants in the neighborhood ta see whether or not we could get some sort of a lead for Wednesday night's dinner crowd. I got what she was wearing from the scene so's I can ask around. Don't have a picture but ya never know, somebody might know somethin'."

"Yes, you're certainly right. Good luck and good night."

"See ya, Dom," Jackson gave one last look at the corpse then turned to go shaking his head. Jackson reached into his coat pocket and pulled out his bottle of TUMS Extra Strength. He opened it, shook out a few tablets, popped them in his mouth and closed the bottle with a snap.

Vitalli was going to say something to his friend, then decided against it, shook his head and watched the man leave the morgue.

He returned to work after the detective left. Vitalli gave the naked body a final wash from all the probing and invasive study his instruments and chemicals did on it being careful not to disturb the small frame he worked on. Drying the still form on the table he said in a barely audible voice, "Goodnight." He whispered bending over the body, "Sleep in peace, my dear, dear one." He tagged the body's large toe with the case number and covered the dead woman with a white sheet.

Next, he wheeled the corpse over to the wall containing the receptacles, opened one and gently

60

transferred the body onto the metal slab. He marked the receptacle with a notation of the case number. He uncovered her face and caressed her hair one last time before replacing the white sheet. Vitalli rolled the metal slab into the wall, closed it securely and walked to the door. He removed his surgical gloves and threw them in the biohazard receptacle. He thoroughly scrubbed his hands and wiped them. He turned off the overhead light and left the morgue as he pulled the door closed behind him.

***

When he was certain Vitalli had left the morgue, Bobby Pieri checked around the empty facility. He pulled on a set of surgical gloves and unlocked the door entering the room. Making his way to the lab drop-off bin, he rummaged through the lab order slips and found the DNA request form attached to the Jane Doe samples. Bobby retrieved the samples and the slip. On his way out of the morgue, he dumped the sample in the biohazards receptacle then locked the door behind him.

Chapter 9

Thanksgiving Day

Protected behind a tree trunk, he peeked out and watched as she climbed the front steps to the house. *Alison.* He mused how she had grown into the young woman she had become. How many years had it been since he lived on this street? He couldn't remember. He could barely recollect the way to this street from the shelter. The frustration of knowing some things and forgetting others racked his brain. The terrible injuries he had suffered clouded his thinking. *If I could only remember. Is she the key to unlock my past?*

***

At the sound of the doorbell, Alison braced herself not knowing what to expect. The Caldwell's opened the door, and she threaded her way through a curtain of beads at the end of the vestibule. Alison scanned the living room. Strange music played from an unseen source. A pungent odor of incense caused her to hold her breath as the odor threatened to burn her eyes and nostrils.

"Hi, Mom. Hi, Dad. I'm here. Happy Thanksgiving. You've done wonders with the place." Alison rolled her eyes toward heaven.

PINNED FOR DEATH

Stifling a cough, she hugged her parents briefly. "I brought dessert," handing her father a store-bought pecan pie.

Her mother, clad in a tie-dyed floor-length baggy dress, hot-pink headband and fluffy slippers greeted her daughter. "Peace and love, Sunshine. Flower-in-the-Valley greets you with peace and love." The woman held up the two fingers of her right hand in the peace sign. Alison rolled her eyes.

"Mom, your name is Fiona."

"That was my given name, but I've taken a name I feel close to the earth with. Flower-in-the-Valley. Let me take your coat and gloves. It's so cold outside. You must be very hungry. We'll have dinner. I made some special treats."

After giving her mother her items, Alison pulled her father aside. "I see the sessions with Dr. Einhorn are going south."

"We're doing the best we can."

"What about her meds? Does she take them?"

"Yes."

"From what I see, I don't think so. Next dose, check her mouth. Make sure she swallows. Mom isn't dangerous, is she?"

"No, she's the gentle soul she's always been."

"Yeah, right." Alison shook her head.

James Caldwell gave his daughter a sheepish grin and shrugged.

All three stood at the dining table holding hands with bowed heads. Mom intoned. "Let's all give thanks to the earth for our bounty." They sat and made conversation.

"How's your job coming along?"

"Dad, it's really getting exciting. I'm going to be working on a murder case. Can't tell you the details, of course, but I'm gaining great experience."

"A murder case? So soon?"

"Well, I've been at the firm almost three months. So the lawyer I'm working with has confidence in me to do the research on the case."

Mom interjected. "Sound's wonderful, Sunshine. But murder is such a dangerous thing to be involved with. Couldn't you do something else?"

"I'm fine. Really."

Some time passed. They ate in silence until Fiona Caldwell noticed Alison picking at her dinner.

"You're not eating much, dear."

"Mom, it's Thanksgiving. I expected turkey not an unreasonable facsimile of twigs and turds."

"Sunshine, I worked hard on this for you."

Alison sighed. "I'm sorry. I know. You did the best you could, but I'm really not into yoghurt-based mash. Listen, it's getting late and I'm a bit tired from the last few days. I'd like to go home now, if you both don't mind."

"But what about dessert? Don't you want some?"

PINNED FOR DEATH

"No, Dad. I'll pass. You enjoy it, okay?"

Her father left the dining room and brought Alison her coat, gloves and purse along with a bag. He helped her with her things. "Allie, baby. Here's a little something for you when you get home. Don't open it now. We wouldn't want to offend your mother. Okay?"

Alison gave her father a hug and a soft kiss on his cheek. "Thanks, Dad. I really love you. You'll be okay? If there's anything I can do, you'll let me know."

"Yes, honey. I'll be fine."

***

The man watched as Alison left the house and descended the front steps to street level. The wind kicked up threatening to blow back the scarf and expose his face to the elements. He held it close to his face and followed her at a safe distance.

Chapter 10

Monday morning

Stretching and not even attempting to stifle a yawn, Alison Caldwell rose as usual at 6:00 a.m. She showered, dressed and ate a quick breakfast, a buttered croissant and a hazelnut latte. She prepared to begin her day.

While tugging on her boots and zipping them up with a flourish, Alison said, "Sure hope today is better than last Wednesday murder night."

Doing a little dance in front of her mirror, she sang, "The only good thing about Wednesday was Officer Mick Hedley. Oh, Mick, oh Mick, how wonderful you are. You're so kind and gentle with those unbelievable blue eyes. You give me goosies all over. I hope I see you again. Omigod! It would be the ultimate, to work with him."

Back to reality, "And Thanksgiving. Having dinner with Mom and Dad. Mom, for once, roast a bona fide, honest-to-Christ, real turkey, not some soy-based thing with gross yoghurt shit poured all over it and you calling it gravy? Please? At least Dad bought me some deli turkey and trimmings. Thanks so much."

Alison gave herself one last check of her makeup in the hall mirror before leaving for her office at the law firm. Satisfied, she cinched her coat's belt securely around her small waist and left the apartment. When she passed the mailboxes, she noticed a white envelope sticking out of her mail slot. She thought nothing of it as she pulled the envelope out of the slot. There wasn't a return address, just her name and address scribbled on the front. As she left the building, Mr. Kelly, the landlord, stopped her.

"Hey, Alison. Oh, I see ya got that letter some guy left for ya. He said it was important."

"Oh, hi, Mr. Kelly. Really?" She held the envelope.

When he turned to leave, she stopped him. "Wait a minute. He? He who?"

"A strange-lookin' fella. Real tall, dark hair, nice storm coat and all. Smelled musty, though, like he was wearin' some kinda stale cologne."

"Did he give you his name, or say where he's from?"

"No. But he seemed to know you, though. Secret admirer?"

"No-o. At least I don't think so. But, thanks," she smiled to herself. She ripped open the letter to find a message written in scraggily script. It read:

Alison. I saw U at murder scene. Yew told it 2 poleece. Wrong thing to do. I followed U home.

Watch out. Yew will b next!

Her stomach lurched and she tasted her morning croissant and latte a second time. She followed Kelly into his office.

Oh, shit! This must be some sort of a joke. Some guy sent me a letter? About the murder? Is this from the killer? And he followed me home? Oh, God. Help.

"M-Mister Kelly. When did this guy show up? Do you remember?"

"Let's see—" The elderly man thought while scratching his day-old whitened beard. "Hm-m-m—"

"Mr. Kelly?" Alison urged. "Like it's real important to me. Is there anything else you can tell me about him? What about his face? Was it full? Lean? Any scars? You said he was tall. How tall? Fat? Thin? Exactly when did he give you this letter?"

"Cripes! Yer actin' like the cops."

"Well-l …"

"He came around midnight last night."

"Yeah, yeah, but what did he look like?"

"Gee, Alison, let's see … he looked like a soldier to me."

Panic rippled through her body. "A-a soldier?"

"Yep."

"W-was there anything that stuck out about him?"

"Yeah. He sorta shuffled when he walked and wore a scarf around his face coverin' part of it."

"Not around his neck but on his face?"

"Yep. Like I said. It was a red scarf."

"Did you see which way he went after he dropped off the letter?" Alison urged the elderly man again with her eyes.

"Yeah—"

"And he went—" she prompted him.

"Oh, yeah. He walked toward Orthodox Street, then turned the corner."

"Uh, Mr. Kelly, which way on Orthodox Street?"

"It was left."

"Facing the street, or the house?"

"Uh, facin' the street."

"Are you sure?"

"Yeah, definitely left."

Alison sighed, "Okay. Is there anything else you remember about what he did, or said?"

"Just he knew you, and, uh—" scratching behind his ear this time.

"And what? It's very important."

"Uh, somethin' like, 'Sorry I', I mean he, 'missed you.' Somethin' like that. He gave me the envelope, I stuck it in your mailbox, and he went away. Why?"

Alison refolded and stuffed the letter back into the ripped-open envelope, and jammed it in her purse. She tried to think of something to say. All she could come up with was, "Uh, because it's bad news."

"Bad news? Sorry to hear it, Alison. Is there anythin' I can do to help?"

"All I can tell you, Mr. Kelly, is this guy is part of the bad news."

Kelly gave Alison a quizzical look as she left the apartment house to go to work.

Oh, holy shit! Now *what do I do? I don't believe this. I have a psycho on my tail. 'Cause I reported Regina Costello's murder to the police. Oh, God!*

Alison muttered. "If I tell someone about it would they believe me? Or should I just keep quiet about it? What the hell should I do? I hafta go to work, but I'm scared to go. I don't have any sick time. But I do feel sick. Real sick, like I'm gonna throw up sick. What if this guy follows me to work and kills me? I just love the thought of looking over my shoulder all the time and being scared of everything that moves."

Thanks, Mr. Scary Person. Thanks for scaring the living shit outta me. Yup! And you're doing a real good job of it, too, 'cause I am scared shitless.

Chapter 11

Alison Caldwell ascended the escalator to the Margaret-Orthodox El platform, on the way to Dunbar, Engels and Quinn. The troubled girl pulled out her cell phone and sent a text to her friend, Lakeesha Ellis.

KEESH: C U @ BRK RM @ 10:00. ND 2 TK URGENT!

She pressed SEND and a few seconds later Alison looked down at Lakeesha's answer.

WHAT UP BFF?

Alison responded. **2 SCRD 2 SAY. C YA THEN.**

She slipped the cell back in its sleeve on the front of her purse. As the doors to the El car opened, she quickly entered. Since there weren't any empty seats, Alison stood the entire trip to the 8th Street station.

Alison felt safer standing scrunched together with other commuters on the train, and after some time, stopped looking around her to see if anyone watched her. When the icy fingers of paranoia slowly ebbed, her own thoughts lulled her as the El train made its stops. Finally the train arrived at the underground station. Alison exited the packed train with her heart a bit lighter knowing she made the trip safely. After arriving at the law firm at 8:15 a.m., she took off her coat, hung it on the coat tree behind her desk and booted up the computer to settle in.

Alison completely forgot she had slipped an intramural envelope under Ramirez' door. It contained the printout of the processed files the Wednesday before Thanksgiving. She printed another copy.

When she approached Ramirez's desk to place the copy on it, the lawyer already arrived in her office. She acknowledged Alison's presence with a nod and a brief, "Thank you", totally shocking Alison.

Upon returning to her work station, Alison began attacking the pile of files Ramirez had given her. At 10:00, she went to the break room. Not paying attention to where she was going, Alison practically bumped into Lakeesha.

"Whoo-hoo, watch it girlfriend. You almost knocked me into next week. Takin' lessons from my daddy?"

"Oh, uh, sorry, Keesh."

"So what's with the weird message this morning? What up? Another bout of Ramirez gettin' on your case?"

"No. If anything, she's behaving herself today. She even thanked me for giving her the list of files she wanted. Guess she had a good Turkey Day."

"Then, what is it? Your text really worried me. What up?"

"It's really bad. But I don't think I can tell you everything."

"Whatever it is, you can tell me. You know I won't say nuthin to nobody. Now, please—"

"But my telling you what this is, isn't it conflict of interest or something-or-other? Or corrupting the facts on a case, and—"

Lakeesha interrupted, "Not if the somethin's real bad. Nuh, uh."

"Oh, it's ... it's—"

Tapping Alison's forehead three times, "Yeah. C'mon. I know somethin's goin' on up there, and I'm not lettin' you go 'til you tell me exactly what it is."

"Keesh. I got a letter stuffed in my mail slot at home this morning. Well, actually it came last night, but I found it this morning."

"And—"

"And I opened it."

"So, what did it say?"

"Keesh. It's a threatening letter."

Lakeesha's mouth dropped open. "Huh? You got a threatening letter? From who? What's it say?"

"From who? I asked my landlord, Mr. Kelly, about it, and he told me he got it from a soldier."

"Wait just a damn minute. How do you know a soldier?"

She responded in a harsh whisper, "That's what I was afraid to tell you about. The soldier is someone I saw the night of the murder."

"What murder?"

Almost crying, "Regina Costello's. She's dead, and I found her and this-this soldier guy came out of nowhere, and my phone died calling it in to the police. He wrote me the note, and I don't know what to do."

"Oh, my God! Oh, Allie. Ya gotta tell someone."

"Yeah. I know. Who knows where I live other than you, the other people I work with, and—"

"What did the threatening letter say?"

Alison looked around making sure no one was within earshot to hear her. Close to Lakeesha's face and in an almost inaudible voice, "It said I was in danger and I'm gonna die. The note is from the killer."

"No shit! The soldier killed Regina? Are you sure?"

"Yeah, shit! I'm sure. And it means I'm in very deep shit. What do I do about it, Keesh? What the fuck do I do?"

"Go directly to Ramirez without passin' go or collectin' two hundred bucks."

PINNED FOR DEATH

Exasperated, Alison whined, "Oh, God. I know I was debating seeing her about this all the way into work. But the old bitch'll bite my head off for sure."

"Now, you listen to me. You gettin' this letter ain't your fault. And she's the lawyer workin' on the Costello case, isn't she?"

"Yeah, but—"

"You gotta go tell Ramirez no matter what she does or says. She just might save your tail. You gotta do this, and I'm gonna see to it you do."

"Girls. Girls. This is no time for socializing. By my watch break time is over. Time's wasting. Go back to work." Pat Owens passed both young women outside her office door.

"We're not socializin', Pat," Lakeesha said.

"Oh?"

"We're talkin' serious business here. Alison and I are goin' directly to Carlotta's office right now to straighten things out."

"Oh, God!" Alison whined again.

"C'mon, girlfriend. Get an extra piece of your nerve on, and let's go see her right now."

"What's this all about?" Owens asked.

"Pat, we'll tell ya about it later. Sorry. We're not dissin' ya, but this is somethin' needin' some doin' right here and now." Lakeesha gave Alison a shove. Lakeesha whispered in Alison's ear, "You ain't gettin' away that easy."

Alison, resigned to the fact, rolled her eyes at Lakeesha and led the way to her work station to get her purse.

***

Carlotta Ramirez's brow wrinkled as she reviewed the details of the Costello case, and its particulars made her more than a little upset. She made an unconscious sweep of her graying, frizzy hair with a free hand attempting to smooth back some wayward strands which had come undone from the chignon behind her head. Ramirez's reading glasses dropped from her nose and dangled from a gold chain she wore around her neck and rubbed her forehead.

So this is what really happened to Jeannette Turner.

Ramirez scrutinized the pictures of the victim, both before and after the crime. Reading the file further, she mused, "I remember Jeannette. She was the young girl afraid of her own shadow." Ramirez nodded sadly. "She thought she could make it as a paralegal in our firm. But not quite, from my memory of her." She touched Jeannette's photo gently. "She's the one who left us so abruptly. Jeannette didn't leave. She was killed. How sad. I suppose—"

Ramirez heard a frantic knock at her door.

"Come in."

Alison entered. "Oh, Carlotta. Sorry to bust in on you."

PINNED FOR DEATH

***

Lakeesha stood within earshot of the door trying to hear all the details of what Alison told Ramirez. Pat Owens tapped the girl on the shoulder to get her attention. When Lakeesha turned around to see who it was, Owens mouthed an order to return to her workstation. Lakeesha reluctantly obeyed. Owens crossed her arms over her chest and stayed long enough to make sure Lakeesha returned to her cubicle then Pat returned to her own office.

***

Ramirez looked up. "Oh, it's you. I was about—"

Alison interrupted, very agitated, "Yeah, it's me. Sorry, Carlotta. Don't mean to cut you. I'm in some deep you-know-what. And it's really, really excruciatingly deep."

"Will you please calm down? Remember where you are, young lady. Dunbar, Engels, and Quinn is a most prestigious law firm, and—"

What does she want me to do? Sit up and bark? Or roll over and play dead?

"No, no, no. You don't understand. This is the ultimate in badness," Alison interrupted. "I-I mean this even tops any other mess I ever got myself into. Even as a kid."

Scrutinizing Alison, Ramirez placed her hand on a stack of papers. "Now, please sit down and tell me everything. From the top. I have a lot of work to do."

Alison sat in a chair opposite the older woman's desk and related the experiences of last Wednesday night.

"*O, dios mio!*" Ramirez crossed herself. "Regina Costello is dead? Are you sure the body is hers?" The sudden impact on the lawyer's brain was as if she had been smacked in the face with a bat.

"Yeah. As sure as the boots on her feet. But because there wasn't any ID on the body, the police are still calling her a Jane Doe. My word doesn't mean diddle bop until a positive ID can be made."

The lawyer recovered from the shock. "Alison, it's what happens in a crime investigation. Everything needs to be carefully documented. If there is one slip-up on anything pertinent to a case, it's inadmissible in court. You should realize it from your training. Since no ID was found on the body, she will still be considered a Jane Doe."

"It's what the police told me. Can you believe this? The first case I'm actually researching, and the person directly involved in reopening her brother's case winds up dead in an alley."

"This is terrible."

"Yeah, you got that right. But, what can we do?"

"Alison, I'll need to inform Regina Costello's parents and ask for permission to continue dealing with her brother's situation. This case is becoming more involved than I thought it would be. You gave Officer Hedley all the details as you remembered them? Left nothing out?"

"No, uh, I mean yes. I-I mean I did everything I was supposed to," Alison replied, still flustered. "W-why?"

"Why, what, Alison?"

"Why didn't you tell me about Jeannette Turner being a paralegal who worked with you? You kept the little bit of info from me, and I want to know why."

"I didn't think it would matter."

Alison's voice raised a good two octaves and a few decibels louder, as she screamed, "You didn't think it would matter? Why the hell not? I'm very much involved now. Don't you think you should've clued me in on the fact someone under *your* charge was killed, murdered, in the most rank way, *Ms.* Ramirez?"

Ramirez's face flushed purple. "Will you kindly hush up? Does the entire firm have to know?" She added barely above a whisper. "I suppose you're right. I should've told you about Jeannette."

Alison stomped around the desk. She bent over and stared into the lawyer's face. "You're damn right I'm right. I saw Jeannette's pics. Now Regina is dead too. Am I next? How do I get outta this mess?"

BEVERLY ANN MEYERS

"If you'll be quiet, maybe I can think. First of all, you did the right thing. You went to the police to give them your statement. You're a witness now, and you've been threatened. You need to do this: go back to the police—"

"The police? This creep knows where I live, and maybe even where I work. Guess how I got the letter. He's gonna kill me if I even *step* near a police station again."

"All right! All right. As I was about to say before you interrupted me. You must go to them and tell them about the letter. Tell them you feel threatened, which you most definitely are, and you waited to speak to me before going to speak with them. The letter is evidence that is valuable and helpful to this case. You must show it to the police."

Seeing Alison's frightened look mixed with exasperation, Ramirez added, "Better yet. I'll go with you as your legal counsel."

"Legal counsel? Y-you mean I could go to jail?"

"No. Of course not you foolish girl. Listen to me. I know you're scared. This little tidbit is scaring me, too. Believe me. With my being there with you, you'll be safe. If the police ask you any questions you don't feel you can answer, I'll be there to advise you. This way you won't be putting yourself into jeopardy. You still have the letter, don't you?"

"Yeah. I kept the trophy. Here."

PINNED FOR DEATH

Grinding her teeth, Ramirez banged her fist on the desk. "Listen to me, you irritating little twit. This is serious business we're talking about here. Don't get flippant with me, young lady. You're the one who asked for my help, remember?"

"S-sorry. It's such a pain. A-and I'm so scared. I almost didn't come to work today because of this mess."

"Unfortunately, it's the price one pays for being at the wrong place at the wrong time, and doing the right thing about it. It's something which needs to be done. And immediately. You are in quite a bit of trouble here, and fortunately I can help you get out of some of it."

"Uh—"

"Alison. Uh, what?"

"Uh, do you think the letter was just a prank? You know, a lame prank somebody's pulling on me?"

"But didn't you say your landlord told you the soldier gave the letter to him?"

"Yeah."

"Then it's no prank. This note is a very serious threat and should not be taken lightly."

"I guess you're right. It's—"

"Look, Alison, I know you're scared. The letter will not go away. Believe me. I wish you hadn't been pulled into this. But, unfortunately, you have. So you need to do certain things to protect yourself, and I'm here to help you. Okay?"

With a very deep sigh, Alison replied, "Yeah. Okay. I guess I gotta do what I gotta do."

"Now, do you have someone who you could stay with until this business blows over?"

"No. I live by myself."

"Where?"

"In Frankford."

"What about your parents? Couldn't you move in with them until this matter blows over?"

"Oh, yeah. Good old Mom and Dad. I can really see myself living with them. When Mom isn't snorting something, she's smoking something else; and when Dad's head isn't watching TV, he lets Mom get away with anything she wants. Me moving back in with them? I don't think so."

"Do you have brothers or sisters to stay with?"

"No. My older brother was killed in Afghanistan four years ago. Mom went hippie on us soon afterwards. She's reliving her second or third teenhood, and Dad's no better."

"I'm sorry to hear."

"Last Christmas I bought Mom amethyst earrings with a matching necklace and you know what she did with them? She hocked them to buy herself a new bong to smoke shit with. And you want me to move back in with them? I *really* don't think so."

Ramirez sighed. "You live in Frankford. I see. Would you mind staying with me? There's an apartment attached to the rear of my house. Now, this is only a temporary arrangement. Is it okay with you?"

Alison eyes nearly popped out of their sockets, "You have an apartment behind your house? A-and you'd let me stay there?"

"Yes."

"Y-you'd do that for me? But, you hate me."

Ramirez sighed again, "I don't hate you, Alison. What I've been trying to do is to mold you into a good paralegal. I've seen the way in which you work. You're very talented, give great attention to detail and most of the time you know what you're doing."

"Oh, and all those files you conveniently left on my desk was to help me polish my data entry skills?"

"No, to clue you in to what actually goes on within a law firm. The clock doesn't rule us, Alison. It's the devotion to one's job which determines how far we will go in life. In our professions. Never forget it, all right?"

"If you say so," Alison said, not really convinced of the lawyer's explanation.

"How does my offer sound now?"

"I have a habit of eating people out of their house and home. I borrow clothes I don't return," Alison warned.

"There will be rules you will follow."

"Of course. There are always rules," Alison answered as she rolled her eyes toward the ceiling.

"Have you always been so outspoken?"

"Uh, guess you could say so. My dad always tells me I have a big mouth. And I say what I think no matter how many times he tells me to shut up."

"Hm-m. You see, Alison. It's the … let us say, quality you possess, my dear, which intrigues me for some reason. Don't know why exactly, but it does. Now back to the issue at hand. You will stay in the apartment attached to the rear of my home. Understood? We come and go to work together. No family, no friends, no loud music. Clear? The connecting door automatically locks after being closed, so you have some privacy and security. And I'll only be one yell away. Fair enough?"

"Are you sure I'm not putting you out?"

"Honestly? Yes, you are, but this is necessary. Besides, you really don't have much choice, do you? You said this lunatic knows where you live. Think about it. You're not safe being by yourself. We're going to the police station. Now."

"Oh, here we go again," Alison rolled her eyes.

Gently giving the paralegal's hand a little pat, "Alison, listen to reason. This needs to be done. You're not safe without some help. I know it, and you know it. After we visit the police station and you give them your formal statement about the letter you

PINNED FOR DEATH

received, I'll come with you to your place to pack a few things. Look, let's leave right away."

"But what about Pat? What do I tell her about leaving the office?"

"Oh, I'll tell her we're out on a case, and we'll be back in a little while. That's all she needs to know."

"B-but my landlord, Mr. Kelly. What should I tell him?"

Ramirez gave a wry smile. "When we go to your apartment, tell him you're visiting your old maid aunt who needs your help for awhile. I know you can concoct a reasonable-sounding story in that brain of yours."

"But, but—"

"No buts about it. My dear girl, the less people know what's going on the better for you. Pat doesn't have to know anything, nor does Mr. Kelly. Let's go."

"Carlotta. How can I ever thank you?"

Ramirez shook her head as she rose from the desk. "I'll think of something to be sure."

Chapter 12

Moving in with Ramirez wasn't better than Alison anticipated, it was fantastic. After all, there were wonderful perks.

"Gee, it's like having my own place. It's so big, and so private. I have my own entrance so I don't hafta bump into Ramirez too often. And it's really a sweet apartment. Totally sweet. I even have my own bathroom," Alison spoke aloud as she admired her new living arrangement. She went to the rear window and admired view. All the hills of Chestnut Hill offered a country feeling. The apartment was large enough to accommodate at least three people.

"I'm really gonna like it here. Ramirez, I do owe you a big thanks for this one. Hope you behave yourself."

She flopped down on the brown corduroy couch and scrunched herself into it feeling its wide, furry wale. She felt so safe and secure.

Nothing and no one can touch me. Mr. Scary Person you can't get me now. I'm here, I'm safe, and I can finally relax after a few days of hell.

A knock on Alison's door woke her from her thoughts.

"Alison? Is everything all right?"

"Oh, yeah. I'll open the door," she called out.

"Well, how's it going?" Ramirez asked at the door.

86

PINNED FOR DEATH

"Carlotta, you're the best. How can I ever thank you? I need to treat you to dinner, or—"

"No, no, no. It's all right. I did this because you were in trouble. And I hope you like it here."

"You know you're making me feel guilty about my living here with you. I'm gonna do something for you that's extra special. And don't fight me on this. You're gonna get what's coming to you. That's a fact.

"I know. I'm gonna treat you to dinner at this little café tomorrow night. I heard about it from one of the other paralegals. Anything you want. It's on me. And I don't want to hear anything in the negateevo about it."

"Alison, let's not get ahead of ourselves. This is a temporary living arrangement until the facts of this case are resolved. And I think dinner, or any other manner of treating, especially at night is, let's say, we'll put it on hold for a while. Understood?" Ramirez looked her guest right in the eye.

"Oh, okay. If it's how you feel about it. By the way, how *is* the Marco Costello case coming I began researching on last Wednesday?"

"There's something I need to tell you about it. Something's really odd about the case. You'll need to see this for yourself. I have the file in my office downstairs. Wait right here, and I'll be back with it."

"What is it?"

"Alison, this is one for the books. I'll be but a second."

Alison felt knots in her stomach beginning to form when she thought of the horrible case of Jeannette Turner.

What the hell did Ramirez find out about the Costello case? I hope we didn't step into the kind of shit nobody gets out of.

Chapter 13

"Alison, here it is," Ramirez said, returning. "Sit down. This case is something that needs to be read while you're sitting down."

"Tell me. God. You have my stomach talking nasty to me."

"Well, read the file. Then tell me what's *really* nasty."

Alison read through Marco's case file. It was something she never expected.

"This says Marco knew a Richard Parker? So?"

"Read on. It gets more and more bizarre."

A bit later after flipping through some pages, "Okay. It goes on to say, by interviewing coworkers, Richard and Marco were seeing a lot of each other."

Ramirez nodded for Alison to continue. But Alison stopped reading.

"So people thought Marco Costello was having an affair with Richard Parker?" Alison scrunched her face. "Gay? He's gay? Why is it all the hunky guys turn out to be gay?"

"Yes. That's exactly what this new information implies, don't you think?"

"But, Carlotta, they could've been only associates, or men-friends, or something. Just because Marco and Richard saw a lot of each other doesn't mean they were hooking up at Jeannette's expense."

"But why were they spending so much time together? Even some of Marco's friends said they were seen together a little too much. How does it sit with you?"

"Marco was gay and cheating on Jeannette? Poor Jeannette. She was caught in the middle."

Ramirez nodded.

"If Marco was gay and Jeannette found out about it, could it be the reason she was killed? Marco had another life and needed to keep it secret? But Jeannette wouldn't hear of it. She was pissed. She threatened to tell his parents. Jeannette and Marco fought over it, and he killed her. Plain and simple. He couldn't come out to his family."

"That's a possibility."

"If it *is* the case, then the right person was sent to prison for Jeannette's murder. Guess it's gonna be a tough one for Regina's family to live with."

"I suppose."

"Okay. This solves *that* mystery. But who wrote me the letter?" It came to Alison in a flash.

"Ohmigod! Richard Parker. He's the soldier. He had to disguise himself so no one would find out he's the killer. Oh, God! Both of us are in real deep shit. Sorry!" Alison raised her hand to her mouth, then quickly took it away, as she continued, "'Cause we both know what really happened, and Richard's gonna find out and kill us."

"Alison, let's not jump to conclusions."

PINNED FOR DEATH

"But who else could've killed Regina? The only other person involved is Richard Parker. He's the killer, and ... uh, oh! Wait a minute. Do you think they were in this thing together? Marco and Richard? Maybe *both* of them killed Jeannette when she confronted them about their affair. Richard pinned the crime on Marco. Marco was convicted, sent to prison while Richard got away with it.

"Or ... or, maybe Jeannette confronted both guys, and she was killed by accident. No, doesn't sound right. No, I still like the idea both of 'em killed Jeannette with Marco going to jail, and Richard getting away with it. It's definitely the way it happened. I'm sure of it."

"Alison, you definitely have quite an imagination. The wheels in your brain are certainly spinning on this case. You think just like a detective. Maybe you're in the wrong line of work."

"Yeah, right. I can just about detect how to get home."

Ramirez laughed and shook her head.

"Carlotta, how did you get this info about the affair?"

"Well, we're really not certain Marco was having an affair with this Richard Parker person, but from the information, it's beginning to look like it. I did some checking about who attended the insurance conference in Baltimore. Since I needed a document either proving or disproving Marco attended the conference, I was able to speak to the manager of the insurance company. She gave me what I needed. I also spoke to the director of the conference's assistant who gave me some names of people Marco frequented with, and I checked these people out who corroborated what Regina Costello had told me. I was allowed to have a copy of the attendees' sign-in sheet."

"Was Marco there? I mean did he sign a register, or something?"

"Yes, he did. The copy proves it."

"Okay. So we have evidence of his attendance. But did he stay there, at the conference, I mean? And did Richard Parker stay there, too? You know, they could've snuck out early and had enough time to kill Jeannette Turner and return to the conference like nothing happened."

Alison realized what she had said as a sickening feeling crept into her stomach, "Oh my God, this is really creepy. Richard is still around. And as for Regina, she was killed because she figured out about Richard, too. He killed her because she reopened Marco's case, and it would implicate him. I mean Richard. So she had to die. Oh my God! Did you go to the medical examiner's office?"

"Yes. But the ME didn't give me any hard evidence Richard Parker's involved."

Alison responded, "Parker covered his tracks pretty well. Eventually he'll trip himself up. There has to be something connecting Parker with Jeannette and Regina's murders. There has to be. And I know we'll find it. You and me. Yes, we will. This is so positively rank. Thanks so much for letting me stay with you. I do feel safe living here."

"I'm glad I'm able to help. Now after all this excitement, how about we both turn in. It might be a long day at the office tomorrow."

Chapter 14

At her desk, Alison opened the file Ramirez had given her and read Marco Costello, thirty years of age, had been accused of murder. She noticed a glossy, 8x11-color picture of him. She picked it up, and couldn't help herself as she studied the face of the convicted murderer of Jeannette Turner. Alison mused over his features: the prominent forehead, medium-brown hair, deep-set dark brown eyes, an aquiline nose, and what also struck her his crooked smile. A smile suggested mirth and concealing secrets, but certainly not the face of a man who would willfully take someone's life.

The victim, a woman, in her early twenties was found dead, but her identity was not able to be determined. The body didn't have any identification. But what had convicted Marco Costello as the killer was a gold initial pin. The pin, with the initial "J", was affixed to her coat. A similar pin with Marco's initial was found on his overcoat. By the time Turner's body was found, it was horribly decomposed. Some of the pictures in the file made Alison taste bile in the back of her throat.

Ugh! How awful. So it looks like the stickpin is the only connection here. You're still the main man, Marco.

Without identification on the body, her identity had remained a mystery until dental records were finally obtained. Reading further, Costello had stated he was not in Philadelphia when the murder took place, but he had been attending an insurance convention in Baltimore, Maryland.

Alison looked at her watch. The time was 1:00 p.m. "Time to grab some lunch. Gonna pick up Keesh."

***

Lakeesha Ellis and Alison found a table in a secluded corner of the Lunch Spot. After the server took their orders, Alison clued Lakeesha about the Costello case.

"Keesh, this case is really bugging me."

"Ya know, I can't get involved too much. But, I can give ya some suggestions on how to approach investigating certain things. Tell me what's got you so uptight."

"Hm-m. It's like this: The guy's sister told us she knows he's innocent. But isn't it what they all say? Of course she'd say so; she's his sister. In his testimony, Costello said he was at the insurance convention, but Baltimore is only two hours away from Philly."

"Yeah, that's right."

"If Costello thought this out carefully, he could've attended the conference for his alibi, made sure his buddies saw him there, slip out of the convention, come back to Philly, kill Turner, dispose of her body and could've had plenty of time to return to the conference. All within, I guess, five, six hours. Don't they have breaks at these things? Long lunches and stuff? Marco could've paid somebody to cover for him, when really he was here in Philly killing poor Jeannette."

"Sure they do. Happens all the time. By the way, when your ninety days are up, you're gonna have a training session where you can pick and choose the sessions ya find interesting to whatcha workin' on."

"Sounds good, but let's get back to this case. Do you think one of Costello's friends killed her? But why? Why would someone you know kill your girlfriend? Jealousy? Revenge?"

"Don't know, girlfriend."

Alison paused for a moment, furrowed her brow then continued. "If this friend had the hots for Jeannette wouldn't he want to kill Marco instead? But, doesn't the evidence point to Marco, not anyone else? Jeannette could've been seeing someone else, decided to break off their relationship, and that's why Marco killed her. Why does my gut says something smells about this?"

"Oh, Allie, it's nothing. Get a grip."

Their orders came. They stared at each other as they munched on Philly cheese steaks, fries and Oreo cookie milkshakes.

PINNED FOR DEATH

Between bites of food, Lakeesha remarked, "Allie, your makin' too much of this case, and ya know it."

***

After lunch with Lakeesha Ellis, both young women returned to the law office. At her desk Alison found, dumped in the in box, several files needing her prompt attention. She looked over the signed slips on top of each file.

I have been Ramirized. Shit! Look at this mound of crap. How about a shitload of shit *in your Christmas stocking, Ramirez?*

Alison noticed Ramirez's office door was open and she strained to see whether or not the lawyer was gloating at Alison's expense, but the poor girl couldn't determine whether or not it was true. The narrow opening of her cubicle was too far away from Ramirez's office, and she felt it was too risky to attempt to get a good look at Ramirez's face.

Nah, it's hardly worth the effort. But anyway. Maybe this is a good thing. I'll gain more experience. Watch your back real *good, Ramirez.*

While she was engrossed in processing the files, Alison heard Ramirez's office door close. As Ramirez strode past Alison's cubicle, Ramirez called out to her with a flourish, "Time to pack up. Don't forget to initial the work you've finished and place them in the confidential file drawer. Tomorrow, I want to see a printout of all the files you've processed on my desk."

Alison didn't look up, but scribbled her initials on the completed work. "Okay, let's go."

PINNED FOR DEATH

Chapter 15

One week later in the break room.

Lakeesha Ellis casually asked Alison. "By the way, how's it goin' stayin' with Ramirez?"

"Everything's great. You should see her home. It's the most magnifico house I've ever seen. There are three full-size bathrooms—one on each floor. Now get this. I have my own apartment. It's so big. I can't believe it. It's attached to the back of her house. I even have my own entrance. It means I can sneak anybody in without her knowing a thing. Hint, hint, hint."

"I hear an invite."

"Why not? Nobody's supposed to know I'm living there. And with my private entrance, Ramirez won't find out. Right?"

"Right! Say, Allie, whatcha doin' tonight after work?"

"You mean after I finish that pile of files Ramirez dropped on my desk? Nothing, really."

"Okay, then. Meet me downstairs in the main lobby at 5:30, and—"

"And?" Alison's eyes twinkled.

"I'm gonna get you to do a little fun after you finish."

"Did you say fun?"

"Yeah. How 'bout the Back Draught?"

"Oh. It's the place I was supposed to meet you on murder night Wednesday. So you want to go there after work?"

"Yep. That's not a problem, is it?"

"Well, you know the reason I'm staying at Ramirez's don't you. And I'm supposed to go home with Ramirez after work."

"You're a big girl. Tell her you wanna get a handle on some of the files she gave you. And tell her I'll take you home."

"Sounds good, but—"

"Yeah, so? What's with the hesita— Oh, you think that guy is gonna come after you?"

"Well-l, the scary letter I found in my mailbox, you know, Mr. Spooky Guy. It's lingering on my brain. I don't know—"

"Look, we'll be together, okay? Allie, don't put yourself in a box. We're goin' out tonight, and we're gonna have some fun. Anyway, I know the bouncer in this place who can punch your Mr. Spooky Guy's lights out with one turn of his fist if he ever tries anything on you. And, I know some *karatay* moves. Maybe you should look into takin' some *karatay* lessons yourself. C'mon, girlfriend. Don't back down. Okay?"

With a sigh, Alison agreed. "Oh, okay. You win. I'll tell her."

"Well, then you're in for a real treat."

"Speaking of treats, I'm buying."

"No way. This is strictly on me, and I'm not takin' no for an answer," Lakeesha saw the wide-eyed look of protest on Alison's face and added, "Look, Allie, I'll cut you a deal. This time it's my treat. Next time it's yours. Okay?"

"Well, it's okay, I guess. But why?"

"'Cause you're gonna show me that big beautiful house afterwards, aren't ya?"

"Okay. Tonight it's your treat. But I'm holding you to next time. Deal?"

"It's a done deal. See ya later."

"See ya at 5:30 sharp," Alison said as her friend left returning to her cubicle.

Maybe Keesh is right. I shouldn't live in a box. "Okay, Mr. Spooky Guy, I refuse to let you get to me. And one more thing, if you're really Richard Parker, I'm coming after you with lots of ammo."

Chapter 16

The Back Draught the same night around 6.00pm

Lakeesha and Alison entered the bar and grille. Loud music pulsed from sound equipment. The place was dimly lit, smoky, and smelled of stale beer threatening to give the newcomers an instant buzz from the odor. People were crowding around the stage set up in the rear. After Lakeesha paid the cover charge, they hung up their coats on the coat rack beside the entrance to the bar.

One young girl, barely out of her teens, swayed and twirled in time to the music. It was early and the regular crowd hadn't shuffled in.

Since Wednesday nights were devoted to karaoke, an inebriated man in his early forties serenaded the clientele. He thought he could sing Billy Joel's *Piano Man*, but in reality sounded more like nails on a chalk board. Every time he swung his hips, attempting to keep in time with the rhythm of the song, he teetered closer to the edge of the stage. The video screen mimicked his movements, making the performance only more comical. His captive audience gave him the usual jeers and whistles. He ignored their attacks on his laughable attempt at singing.

PINNED FOR DEATH

"Keesh, look at the idiot up on stage. He looks like such a complete dork."

"The dork you're referring to is one of our junior partners. The poor excuse for a lawyer, girlfriend, is Thomas A. Humphrey. I'm sure the 'A' stands for asshole," Lakeesha sneered. "Bastard made my life miserable for four months on the Compton case I was workin' on. What a total turd."

Humphrey turned to the side with a quick jerk. Alison broke out in guffaws.

"Allie, whatcha doin'?" Lakeesha watched Alison reach into her purse and whisk out her cell phone, aimed and pressed a button activating the video option.

"Ha, ha, ha! It's called blackmail. If Thomas Asshole gives you any more flack, show him this. Okay, Thomas baby. Smile for the camera." A bright light from Alison's cell caught the man leaning back with microphone in hand as if he were going to ingest it much like a sword swallower.

"Wasn't there a movie called *Deep Throat* 'way back in the Dark Ages?"

Lakeesha answered. "Yes. But you can call this guy Deep Mike."

"Don't make me laugh anymore. My stomach is killing me, ha, ha, ha! I'm sure glad this guy has a day job, 'cause he sure sucks at night. You know, you could download this video on to your computer.

Every time Suckin' Humphrey comes around you could show it to him."

"It'd be going a little too far, don'tcha think?"

"Well—"

"Girlfriend, you're one bad puddy."

"You know it."

Lakeesha Ellis couldn't contain herself and joined Alison in uncontrollable laughter.

"Glad you're having such a good time, Allie."

"Yup! If I ever meet him in the office, I'll always remember him this way. It's too indelibly etched on my brain. I hope any other singers after him are at least a little better on the ears. Oh, God! His voice sounds like he stepped on a cat in heat."

Lakeesha nodded.

When the man finished, he attempted to bow to the audience, but stumbled nearly falling off the stage. Both women sighed with relief. The audience gave Humphrey some catcalls as he left.

The next singer was a young girl who sang a professional-sounding rendition of Bonnie Raitt's, *Something to Talk About*. When she finished, her audience applauded her profusely.

"Hey, I got an idea."

"What're you gonna do?"

"Watch and listen, Keesh. Could you hold my purse?" Alison made her way to the side of the stage. She whispered into the emcee's ear. He nodded. She climbed the two steps on to the stage while he announced her name telling the audience she was going to sing a cover of Avril Lavigne's, *Keep Holding On.*

At first, Alison felt intimidated on the stage with everyone staring at her. *No suspicious characters as far as I can see. Well, here goes.*

When the music began and the introduction of the song was well under way, she proved to be in her element as she entranced the audience.

She assured herself everyone appeared to be legit. Alison continued singing adding some of her own flourishes. When done, some guys in front of the stage gave her a standing ovation, some others in the back whistled.

When Alison returned to the bar picking up her purse, a shocked Lakeesha asked, "Where the *hell* did you learn to do that? Sure you're not Avril's sis?"

"I don't know, I just open my mouth and it comes out."

"You open your mouth and it comes out. Yeah, right. I don't know about you. Sure you wanna be a paralegal all your life? All I can say is Avril better watch her back, girlfriend. After that performance, I'm *definitely* treatin' you tonight. Let's get some refreshment."

Alison blushed. "Thanks, Keesh."

Lakeesha grabbed the bartender's attention, noticed his, 'Hi, I'm Jimmy!' tag on his shirt. "Hey,

Jimmy? Jimmy. Yeah. Over here. Two Bud Lights, for my friend the rock star and me, please."

"No prob, young lady. Mighty fine singin' there." Jimmy opened the bottles and handed them over to Lakeesha. Alison blushed again.

"Thanks, Jimmy," Lakeesha answered. She slapped a bill on the bar and gave Jimmy a sweet smile as she took the beers from the bar.

"Are you sure you can do this, Lakeesha? I mean I'm perfectly willing to—"

"No, no, no, this is my treat. I told you, you deserve it for what you're doing for me. You're gonna show me where you live. And it deserves at least a coupla beers and some wings? Let's go find a table so we can sit and have a chat.

"Oh, shit!"

"What's up?" Alison asked.

"Him is what's up."

"Him, who?"

Lakeesha nudged Alison with her elbow. "None other than—"

Alison looked in the direction her friend was motioning with her chin. Lakeesha almost tripped over her own feet. "Bobby Pieri, the Hunk. Oh, my God. Allie, quick. Into this booth before he sees us," Lakeesha urged her friend, giving her a shove into the leather seat. Poor Alison flopped into the seat not knowing what to make of the man Lakeesha was attempting to avoid. Lakeesha hoped the bar's dim lights would shield them from the unwanted intruder.

Bobby Pieri walked to the bar eyeing Jimmy. When Jimmy acknowledged him with a quick nod, Bobby lowered his head as if something was weighing on his mind.

"Hey, buddy. Want your usual?" the bartender asked. "Here's your Yuengling."

"Yeah. Why not? Say, uh, how's the action here tonight?" Bobby asked after taking a long gulp of his beer.

"For a Wednesday, it's not too shabby."

Wiping his mouth with the back of his hand he said, "Thanks for the liquid refreshment."

Jimmy noticing Bobby's odd behavior, lowered his voice, asking, "Bobby is everything all right? You look a bit peaked."

Bobby shuddered, "I got a bit o' bad news last week."

"Oh? It's not your girl, is it? She's okay, isn't she? You look a little green around the gills."

Bobby shook. "I guess I'm comin' down with some sort of bug."

"Well, 'tis the season for coughin' and sneezin'. Is your girlfriend okay? As soon as I mentioned her, you took a turn for the worse."

"Look, Jimbo, she's really not my girlfriend. She's well taken care of, for sure," Bobby Pieri trembled as he spoke. He sighed, "She's probably restin' comfortably, I'm sure. So's I'm by myself now."

"You gave me the impression she was your girlfriend. You were talking a lot about her. And I thought she was your special girl."

"Oh, uh, she's just, uh, somebody I knew."

"Knew?"

"I-I mean know. Someone I know, is all."

"I see," Jimmy said. "Maybe you should call 'er to see if she's all right."

"N-no. I'm sure she's okay."

"If you say so, buddy. Remember, I'm always here to talk. Or hear a confession."

Bobby's eyes flashed. He hunched over the bar and pushed his face close to the bartender's, "Jimmy, I think it's the end of that tune. She doesn't have anything to say about how I spend my free time, okay? By this time, she's all wrapped up nice 'n cozy, tight as a drum. She knows I come and go as I please. And make the next one a frebbie, too. Understand?"

With his hands in the air, Jimmy backed away from Bobby, "Uh, sure, Bobby. Anything you say". He opened another Yuengling. "I think you better move along, buddy."

Jimmy searched the far end of the room and spotted one of the bouncers. He caught the man's attention and signaled him with a slight nod of his head to approach the bar.

PINNED FOR DEATH

Bobby turned around in time to see Lakeesha and Alison chatting in their booth. When he came toward them, they stopped talking.

"Well, well, well. Hello lovelies. And what do I owe my bumping into such special people?" A crooked grin spread across Bobby's face.

"Hi, Bobby," Lakeesha glared at him.

"What's a matter, Lakeesha? Have something against seeing an old friend?"

"Look, Bobby, you're not my friend anymore. What we had is in the past and was a lot of fun, but it's over. Okay? Why don't you take your beer and leave us alone? You're interrupting a private conversation. Now, go. Please?"

Bobby walked closer to Lakeesha and brushed his free hand over her cheek. She closed her eyes, pressed his hand with hers. She whispered. "Bobby, baby, you know I really wanted you. It didn't work out. It just didn't work out." She sniffed. "Maybe in another life, sweetie." Lakeesha kissed his hand then released her hold on it. He walked away.

Concerned, Alison placed a hand on Lakeesha's shoulder. "What was that all about?"

"I don't want to spoil the evening. I'll tell ya some other time. Okay?"

"If it's what you want. Sure."

Lenny, the bouncer, saw what happened and came over to the booth. "Is everything okay over here?"

Alison offered. "Yeah. We're good."

Lenny returned to his station.

Lakeesha wiped a tear from her eye. "Let's order some wings."

Alison placed a hand on her friend's shoulder. "Think you can splurge for a double order?"

"Why not? Sounds great. I worked up a fierce appetite."

Chapter 17

Back at Alison's apartment behind the Ramirez home.

"C'mon, Allie. Open the damn door, will ya? I think I hafta pee again."

"Keesh, I would if only the damn door would stop moving."

"C'mon, you can do it, baby." Lakeesha crossed her long, lean legs.

"Shhhhhh! You'll wake up Ramirez. If she finds us wasted like this, she could throw me out on my ass."

Lakeesha cheered at the successful try. Both young women laughed and snorted. When the door opened, Alison felt the wall trying to find the light switch. When she finally did, she flipped the switch and fell face first on the living room floor. Lakeesha practically fell on top of her, but caught herself by holding on to the door frame.

"Ooooo! Ooooooo! Ooo! Oh, God! The light. Gotta turn off the damn light. It feels like it's sawing right through my brain. Keesh, turn down the light. It's a dimmer switch."

"Oh, God! I feel like I'm about to puke up my guts. We shoulda ordered those wings. They would've sopped up the beer in our veins. How crazy are we? Yeah, yeah, the light. Here we go. Where's the switch? Oh, never mind. I'm feelin' it. Got it." Lakeesha pressed the wall switch to dim the lamp but missed her footing and almost knocked the table lamp over. Alison grabbed it at the last second, saying, "Close call."

"Where's the baffroom?" slurred Lakeesha.

"It's right down the hall an' to your left."

"Gotcha." Lakeesha, half ran, half stumbled down the hallway. Alison noticed the light go on, and heard the toilet flush. When Lakeesha turned the light out, coming out of the bathroom, she lost her balance and knocked over a standing lamp at the end of the hallway. It landed with a crash.

"Oh, crap. Ramirez heard that. I know it. Now, I'm in really deep shit."

"Sorry, Allie."

"Oh, it's not your fault. It's both our faults. Fault. What-ev-er."

Both of them started laughing again. They stopped when they heard a muffled voice. The voice grew louder and more distinct which gave both women pause.

"Shhhhhhhh. Shhhhhhh. Allie. If we're quiet, maybe she'll go away."

"Heheheh. Are you kidding me? Ramirez never goes away. She keeps goin' like the bunny from the battery commercial. She keeps on goin' and goin' and goin'—"

PINNED FOR DEATH

"Alison? What's going on in there? Who's in there with you? You know the rules. Open up. Open up this instant." Ramirez shouted through the locked door, while pounding on it with her fist.

"Yeah, yeah, yeah. Keep a lid on it, lady. I'm comin'," Alison shouted back. She flicked on another light, winced as her aching head throbbed from the abrupt brightness of the room. On unsteady legs, she stumbled to the door and managed, with great difficulty, to turn the lock and open the door.

Ramirez came barreling into the room, wearing a hot-pink flannel robe with matching fuzzy slippers almost smacking Alison against the wall.

"Alison, Alison Caldwell! Do you know what time it is?"

She squinted at the dial of her watch. "Yeah. It's twelve thirty. So?"

"So? It's late, and you're drunk."

"No, I'm a little buzzed, is all. Ooh! Could ya turn down the color of your robe, please? It's hurting my eyes." Alison shielded them with both hands while giggling.

"More like plastered, I'd say," Ramirez shook her head in disapproval. Looking down the hall, Ramirez added, "And my lamp. You broke my lamp."

"Look, I'll buy you another one, okay?"

"You can't."

"And why not?"

"Because it was an antique."

"Oh. So sorry."

Lakeesha groaned. "Uh, could ya keep it down? My head is swimming."

"Lakeesha Ellis. I'm surprised at you. What the hell were both of you thinking tonight? You're both disgusting. I won't stand for this under my roof. Look at you. Drunk beyond belief." Ramirez gritted her teeth and continued. "Alison, if you weren't in such trouble, I'd throw both of you out on your ears. Out at all hours on a week night, no less."

"Look, Ramirez, you're not my mother. I'll come and go where I want, when I want. Get it?"

"Like hell you will after this little escapade. I took pity on you. I gave you sanctuary. From now on you're definitely coming and going to work with me. I brought you into my home. My home. Do *you* get it?" Ramirez spat.

"Yeah, I get it. But I'm twenty-two years old," Alison spat back.

"More like twenty minus the twenty-two is how you're acting right now, young lady. This is disgraceful behavior. Under my roof, no less."

"We were very careful coming home, Carlotta."

"It's no excuse. And you, Lakeesha. I'm surprised at your behavior. Driving under the influence. I always thought you were mature. Now look at you. What do you think you were doing?"

"Look. We were out havin' some fun," Lakeesha explained with a flourish of her hand.

"Putting yourselves and others in jeopardy is having some fun, I see? Dunbar, Engels and Quinn is a prestigious law firm. We employ people with exemplary conduct."

"Really?" Alison asked.

"Really," Ramirez exclaimed.

"Well, how's *this* for *exhemplry* conduct for ya? Huh?" After the third try, Alison opened her cell phone and shoved the video of Thomas Humphrey gyrating in a most lewd manner under the older woman's nose.

Almost choking on her words, Ramirez gasped, "Whaa-aa? My, God! Where did you ever get that?"

"I took it when Jiggle Hips Humphrey here was performing at the Back Draught tonight. Whaddya think of him now?"

Ramirez couldn't contain her anger. "That bastard. I've worked for the firm for twenty-five years trying to become partner, and the little sniveling fool Humphrey was hired two years ago, and became partner within eighteen months. That-that-that … dick!"

Alison pointed at the man dancing on stage, "As a matter of fact, if you look real close, you can actually see the outline of his—"

Ramirez's voice boomed as she shook with rage. "Alison Caldwell. It's quite enough. Spare me the details of his anatomy. Shut the hell up, will you."

"Carlotta. I've been working at DEQ for almost two years, and I never heard you curse once." Lakeesha emphasized her shocked tone.

"Never mind what I say, or don't say."

"Keesh, there's a first time for everything," Alison put in.

"Done. You're done. Both of you. Come with me, now. Give me your phones. Now."

"Huh? Our phones? Why?" They asked in unison.

"Dammit! Just give them to me … it's your … punishment. No phones. No noise." Ramirez held out her hand. The young women reluctantly gave up their cells.

"Where're we going?" They asked.

"You're sleeping under my supervision. There's a bedroom next to mine. You'll both sleep there. Before work tomorrow, both of you will clean up the mess you made. I'll drive all of us to work together."

"But what about my car?"

"Lakeesha, you're getting on my last nerve. Forget about your damn car."

"Oh, Gawd. My head," Alison moaned.

"If you don't move, more will be hurting than just your head. Now, move it."

116

PINNED FOR DEATH

Alison raised the middle finger of her hand right in Ramirez's face.

"Do it again, and I'll break your finger off."

"Bitch," Alison snarled.

Ramirez raised her hand and slapped Alison across her mouth.

"Screw you. One of these days, you'll get yours." Alison shouted. More softly, "You got one helluva right, lady." Alison gingerly touched her face and moved her jaw up and down.

"Enough of your insolence. Now move." Ramirez shouted.

Alison finally obeyed.

Lakeesha followed both women through the connecting door careful not to stumble. She got her wish, but not the way she wanted. When Ramirez turned on the overhead light, as dim as it was, Lakeesha's eyes narrowed. What she saw through those bleary eyes made her sober up quickly. This part of the house was as magnificent as Alison said it was to the last detail. From the dim light, Lakeesha observed fine furnishings, most likely antiques. Original oil paintings adorned the walls, and beautiful oriental rugs graced highly polished parquet floors.

Lakeesha looked amazed. *Mm—mm—mm—mm—mm! Is this how lawyers live? I'm sure missin' out on the good life. This is definitely for me.*

Ramirez led the way to the bedroom for Alison and Lakeesha. After turning on the overhead light in the room, Ramirez whisked off a puffy, down coverlet. Next, she went over to a dresser, opened a drawer and pulled out two nightgowns handing one to each girl.

"Here. Get out of your clothes and put these on," she ordered.

She ushered both young women into the bedroom. "Come in, you two. This is where you both will sleep tonight. Get right to bed now. I don't want to hear anything from either of you until tomorrow morning. Do you hear me?"

"Uh, Carlotta. It is tomorrow morning."

"Lakeesha, don't *you* smart mouth me," Ramirez warned.

"Yes, ma'am. Sorry."

"I'm waking you up at 5:30 and giving you some towels. Then, both of you get to work to clean up the broken lamp before breakfast. Understand?"

"Yes, Carlotta," they answered.

"Good night, then. I'm right next door." Ramirez, flicked off the overhead light, left the room and slammed the bedroom door.

"Well, that sure didn't earn us any brownie points," Lakeesha undressed and slipped into a nightie.

"Nope. Sure didn't," Alison agreed. "Guess we better get some shut eye."

Alison struggled with the nightie and realized why when she looked down at her hands. She looked as though she had shrunk inside the gown. The sleeves fell way past her hands, and its length fell in folds around her ankles. Lakeesha's gown fit her body, but the length was too short. Her arms stuck out as if she were wearing a child's garment. They looked at each other and laughed as they stripped and threw the gowns on the floor.

Alison stopped laughing. "Nuh, uh. That didn't work at all."

"Nope."

"I feel weird sleeping in my underwear."

"Well, we don't have to." Lakeesha grinned.

"That's getting a little kinky, don't cha think?"

"Yeah. Guess so. Underwear it is. Who's gonna see us, anyway?"

"Nobody but us." Alison giggled, as she and her friend slipped under the covers.

Ramirez shouted, "Shut up in there."

There was silence, then—

Lakeesha asked in a husky whisper, "Allie?"

Alison whispered back, "Yeah?"

"Do you believe Ramirez's mouth tonight when she saw Humphrey dancin' in the video you took of him?"

"Keesh, she was so-o-o pissed. I thought her eyes would pop from her head."

"Yeah, but I feel bad for her. Ya know her tryin' to become partner in the firm."

"Yeah, guess you're right. Guess it's why she's in a funk all the time. But gee, if she is working for the firm for so long and hasn't become partner, why is she still there? Why hasn't she gone lawyering elsewhere and make a new start?"

"Benefits," Lakeesha yawned.

"Benefits?"

"Don't know what the perks are for lawyers, but they hafta be pretty good, if Ramirez's still at the firm. The longer you work at DEQ, you'll get to know all the ins and outs of the benefits package. You'll see," Lakeesha yawned again.

"Oh, okay. My head's really talking nasty to me." Alison turned on the table lamp beside the bed.

"Yeah, Allie. Mine too. So's my stomach."

"Before we call it a night, I'm getting some aspirin and water for our big heads. And something for your stomach." Alison whipped off the covers.

"Okay. Do think Ramirez'll mind?"

"Tough."

"Okay, tough," Lakeesha shrugged. "Do you know where the baffroom is?"

Alison answered. "Yeah, Ramirez gave me the grand tour of the place when I moved in. It's right next door."

"Okay. Just wanna know in case I need to go pee again."

"Ya know what?" Alison asked.

"No, what?"

PINNED FOR DEATH

"You're a bad puddy, too."

"Yeah. I know, girlfriend." Lakeesha laughed, as she watched her friend get out of bed.

When Alison returned to the bedroom, she found her friend snoring peacefully. Within minutes, Alison followed suit.

***

Ramirez turned on Alison's cell, took a chance and punched in the girl's birth date. The app screen appeared.

Not too savvy with your password.

She tapped the app for the video and looked at it again, enlarging the screen. A man in the audience standing near Thomas Humphrey turned around. "*O, dios mio!*" Ramirez crossed herself. The man's crooked smile almost made her heart stop.

Chapter 18

The next morning

With two bath towels in her hand, Ramirez banged on the girls' bedroom door. "Get up. Now!"

"Uh. Is it 5:30 already?" Lakeesha, groggy from sleep shook Alison awake.

"Who? Wha—"

"C'mon, girlfriend. Time to get up and face Ramirez."

"I wanna take a sick day."

"I know, me too, but I don't think it's a good idea."

Another bout of pounding on the door, and Lakeesha quickly got out of bed, picked up a nightie to cover herself and opened the door.

Ramirez rushed into the room and plopped both towels on the bed. "Hurry up. Get washed and dressed. I want to see both of you downstairs in the kitchen."

"What about the broken lamp?"

"Lakeesha, forget about it."

"Forget about the antique lamp? I—"

"Yes, you heard me." Looking at Alison, "And, here's your cell phone." Ramirez tossed it on Alison's side of the bed.

"Okay, thanks. And a good morning to you, too."

Ignoring Alison's snide remark, Ramirez ordered. "When you get downstairs, show me the video you took of Thomas Humphrey again."

With her head resting on one hand, Alison looked up at Ramirez. "But, why?"

"I … I, uh, I want to see it again."

Puzzled, Alison shrugged her shoulders, "Okay."

***

"We're here, Carlotta," Alison announced.

"Good. Now please sit down."

Alison opened her cell. "Okay. Here's Humphrey doing his thing."

"Enlarge it and stop it … right there." Ramirez pointed her finger at the screen. "Tell me what you see."

Alison did as the older woman asked. Both girls looked at the screen. Lakeesha recognized the man staring back at them. "Oh, yeah, it's Bobby Pieri right there smilin'."

Without looking Ramirez answered, "No. it's not."

Alison added, "Sure it is. He's the jerk who was bothering us last night."

Lakeesha agreed with Alison. "Listen to me, Carlotta. I know him very well. He's definitely Bobby Pieri. I've known him for almost a year. Yep. That's definitely Bobby."

Ramirez placed an eight-by-ten glossy on the table next to the video. "Here. Look at this photo. Then tell me if you still think it's Bobby Pieri."

Wide-eyed, Alison stared at the photo. "It's Marco Costello. No, it can't be. He's in a coma. In the prison hospital ward."

"At least, it's where he's supposed to be."

"How ... Wait just a damn minute. You got into my cell. That's invasion of privacy. I could get you for this."

"And do what? Listen, Alison, it's a good thing I did. Marco is out of prison. He could be the person after you. Think about it. I did you a favor."

"When we get to work, I'm gonna report you."

"Forget work today. Both of you. We're going to the Roundhouse and report to the police what we have discovered."

Alison's eyes bulged in fear. "The police? B-but the guy with the note. Remember him? He's gonna kill me for sure."

"Calm down. You'll be safe with me."

Alison and Lakeesha exchanged looks.

***

As usual, the Roundhouse buzzed with activity. All three women went to the reception desk. A woman much older than Carlotta Ramirez peered over her bifocals. "May I help you?"

"Yes. My name is Carlotta Ramirez. Here's my card. I am an attorney at Dunbar, Ellis and Quinn. I—"

Alison cleared her throat.

Ramirez glared at her and began again. "*We* would like to see the officers working on a particular case."

"Do you have an appointment?"

"No. But this is of vital importance."

The receptionist rolled her eyes and came close to Ramirez's face. "Aren't they all? Do you have their names? I could see if they are available."

Alison spoke immediately. "Officers Mick Hedley and Frank Peterson."

"Thank you. Wait a moment, please. I'll buzz them to see if they are free to see you."

With a nod of her head and holding up two fingers, the receptionist instructed them to go to the second floor.

***

After the initial introductions, the women were ushered into an interrogation room. Hedley and Peterson pulled out chairs for Ramirez and the young girls.

Hedley asked. "Why, exactly, did all of you need to see us about?"

Ramirez answered. "There's something very disturbing you need to know about the Regina

Costello murder case. I brought the information with us."

"What about it?"

Ramirez offered. "Marco Costello was convicted of murdering his fiancé, Jeannette Turner two years ago. He was supposedly incarcerated at State Prison in Philadelphia."

"What do you mean by 'supposedly'?"

"This should explain things." Ramirez reached into her valise, pulled out the Costello file, took out Marco Costello's photo and slid it towards Hedley who took a good look. Ramirez prompted Alison. "Give your cell to Officer Hedley."

Alison stared at him.

Ramirez nudged the young girl. "Alison."

"Uh, oh, yeah. Sorry," she answered, retrieving the device from her purse. She opened the phone to the video and stopped it revealing Marco Costello's face. With a nervous smile, Alison showed the stilled video to Hedley.

The officer enlarged the image and looked at Costello's picture. "This certainly changes things. Where and when was this video taken?"

Lakeesha answered. "When we were at the Back Draught last night. I mean Alison and me."

"I see. How do you know Marco Costello?"

Alison answered, "We only know him as Bobby Pieri."

PINNED FOR DEATH

Lakeesha added, "He's an assistant to the ME in Center City. At least it's what he tells everyone."

Peterson asked her. "How long have you known this guy?"

"For about a year."

Hedley said, "We'll take out an APB on him. Thank you for coming in with this evidence. We'll need your phone."

"My phone?"

"Yes, Miss Caldwell. It's evidence now."

Reluctantly, Alison gave her cell to Hedley. "Take good care of it."

Hedley smiled at her remark. "We'll call you when it's okay to pick it up. That's all for now. We'll keep you informed of any further developments."

Alison stared at Hedley again. "That's it? What about the guy with the nasty note?"

"Are you living alone?"

Ramirez offered. "Alison is staying in an apartment behind my home."

Hedley said, "Then you're safe."

Alison gulped and looked at Hedley. *I sure hope so!*

Chapter 19

Later the same day.

Detective Trevor Jackson entered the morgue. His friend, Medical Examiner Dom Vitalli, was deep in work.

"Yo, Dom. Got somethin' ta tell ya about the Jane Doe case yer into."

"What about it?"

"From what Mick tells me, there's a connection with the Jeannette Turner case from some two years ago."

"How so?"

"Our good buddy, Mick spoke with the young woman who called in the Jane Doe murder yer workin' on. The girl mentioned somethin' about findin' a gold pin found on the vic's lapel. I did some checkin' 'cause remember I told ya somethin' seemed familiar about the Jane Doe case that was brought in?"

"Yea-ah."

"Well, as it turned out when Turner's body was found, she had the same pin on 'er coat lapel. The girl who told Mick about it thinks it's a serial killer we're dealin' with."

"Do you know the girl's name?"

PINNED FOR DEATH

"Yeah. Got it right here." Jackson whipped out his notebook, flipped through a few pages and read, "Name's Alison Caldwell."

Vitalli looked up at Jackson. "The pin could just be a trendy thing women wear. As for a serial killing, there's no real evidence of it. Our Jane Doe died from a knife wound in her chest."

Jackson pointed a finger. "My friend, the Turner girl died the same way."

Vitalli adjusted his bifocals and scratched his bearded chin.

Jackson offered. "The pin. That's the only connection. And, another strange thing … Jane Doe was killed two years later than the Turner woman. If we are dealin' with a serial killer, why did the perp wait two years?"

"I haven't a clue."

"Yeah. Exactly what we need … more clues."

Vitalli nodded in agreement. "Apparently they came from different backgrounds. We know Jeannette Turner, a paralegal, lived in West Philly, while Jane Doe, was dressed like an ad from Sachs' or Bloomingdale's. Turner worked for Dunbar, Engles and Quinn, while there's no evidence Jane Doe worked at all. What's the connection between them? Did they somehow know each other? If so, how did they happen to meet?"

Something was missing. The detail eluded them. The thought nagged and nagged like an old crone, poking overgrown nails into their sides, demanding an answer.

Jackson suggested. "Maybe there will be more clues when Turner's body is exhumed, if 'er family and Judge Greenberg allow it."

Vitalli raised his bushy eyebrows. "It would certainly help, if he did. And now to the case of Ms. Jane Doe."

He picked up the large white envelope which had been delivered in the morning. "This sure has been quite a day. I'm exhausted. These late hours are taking their toll on this old bod. I managed to draw the short straw to work on the fiery three-car collision on I-95 south, near the Betsy Ross Bridge."

"Oh, yeah. The one durin' yesterday mornin's rush hour killin' all three drivers."

"Yep. That's the one. One body didn't leave much to work with, and I did my diligent best to sort out corpse from debris. Would you believe I had to pull off a melted cell phone from what was left of the driver's hand?" The ME rolled his eyes and shook his head. "And people still think they can cheat death by taking stupid chances with their lives."

Returning his attention to the as yet unidentified body, he slashed open the envelope with the worn scalpel he always used as a letter opener and pulled out the dental records. The name on the copy was Regina Theresa Costello. He checked deeper into the envelope and found a photograph of the woman before her death who appeared to be in her late twenties. She was more than attractive; she was beautiful with a slight build, long blonde hair and an amazing smile.

Jackson bent down to look at the photo. "What a shame. Such a good lookin' broad."

"And so young. Well, she officially has a name, and Regina Theresa Costello certainly was no broad. What did she do that was so terrible to warrant being murdered?" Looking at the woman's photo, Vitalli spoke. "Did you have a fight with your lover? Did he want to end the relationship after he learned of your pregnancy? Did he know you were pregnant? Were you in the wrong place at the wrong time? And did you know Jeannette Turner? If so, how? What is the connection between both of you?"

"Who knows? Maybe ya can solve her mystery and discover the secrets when the DNA results come back."

Vitalli shook his head as he wrote the Costello woman's name on a label with a Sharpie and stuck it on the file lying on his desk. "Here's hoping." He carefully removed the remainder of the file. "Hey, Becky? Could you please make two copies of this file for me?"

"No prob, Dom. Hi, Trev. How's everything?"

"Ever'thing's jake."

"Good. I'll just be a sec."

Vitalli said, "There's no rush. Our vic isn't going anywhere."

"Sure hope not, guys. Don't want to deal with the walking dead." Becky winked.

After the intern left, Jackson said, "These kids these days. They watch stuff on TV that'll give ya nightmares durin' the day."

Vitally laughed. "That's for sure."

Abruptly, Jackson's cell rang. "Sorry, Dom. Gotta take this."

"It's okay. G'head." Vitally waved at his friend and relaxed in his chair.

Jackson's demeanor abruptly changed from congenial to alarmed when he learned the nature of the call.

"Dom."

"Huh?"

Shaking the coroner awake. "Dom! Anybody else workin' here tonight besides you and Becky?"

A sleepy Vitalli answered. "No."

"Just got wind of one o' them nightmares. Close up shop. I'm drivin' Becky home. An' yer comin' home with me. Now."

Chapter 20

Thursday evening

After work, Carlotta Ramirez dropped Alison off at the house. The lawyer wanted to freshen up for the evening. Then, Carlotta left the house and made her way to Northeast Philadelphia. She headed north on Lincoln Highway to her sister's house in Bensalem, Pa.

She was in the left lane and passed some slower-moving cars on her right. Ramirez needed to get into the right lane in enough time to make it to the Route 1 business cut off. She looked in her rearview mirror and noticed a dark SUV behind her. She clicked on her turn signal to alert the driver she wanted to move into the lane. As she passed into the next lane, the SUV followed her nearly cutting off the car behind it. The smaller vehicle blew its horn and swerved just in time to get out of the van's way.

Jeeze! This guy is a bit impatient. Guess he's going where I'm going. He's getting awful close to me, though. Maybe I should switch back.

After a few minutes, she signaled the van behind her and crossed over into the left lane. So did the van. She did a quick maneuver to the right lane to see if it did the same. Sure enough, it did.

What is it with this guy? Oh, well, he seems harmless. Maybe he's lost.

About two miles later, she signaled again turning off Lincoln Highway onto the bypass. After a little over a mile, she turned off the bypass onto a deserted secondary road which led to the trailer park where her sister lived. The dark SUV was still trailing her coming very close. Too close, in fact.

Dios mio! He's still there? Why is he ... uh. God! He purposely banged right into me. What the hell ... oh! ... does he want?

The SUV following her pulled back.

"Well, maybe the last knock jarred some sense into the idiot."

This time the vehicle sped up.

"What is it with you, you fool. You get way back, you hear me?" *What is your problem?*

"Dammit. I've had it." Carlotta reached for her cell phone which she kept close to the console, but reached out for air instead. The cell had fallen to the floor from the last hit.

"Damn."

She pressed the accelerator and the dark SUV came at her again.

Blam! After this bump, the vehicle behind her retreated again. It stayed at a close distance.

"What is it with you, you bastard? Go away."

It didn't. The van came right up behind her. This time it didn't hit her; its front bumper was touching her car's rear. She pressed down on the accelerator desperately trying to speed away.

PINNED FOR DEATH

"Stop! Don't you get it? Get the hell away from me." She pounded on her horn with a closed fist thinking she could draw attention to someone who might be on the road. She peered into her rearview mirror to see whether or not she could identify something about the person pursuing her. She couldn't. It was too dark on the lonely road which offered no help whatsoever.

The van pulled back, but not so far this time. It was headed straight for her. It sped up faster, and Bang! BANG! BANG!! The SUV gave one last shove and stopped dead.

"God, he's insane. This can't be happening. OOOOOOOOHHHHHHHHHH! AAAAAHHHHHH!"

She screamed as her car was pushed off the road. It crashed into a guidepost and continued into a gully. Ramirez held onto the steering wheel until her knuckles paled from the strain. The vehicle came to an abrupt stop. Ramirez's left arm smashed into the car's door breaking her watch. Bones snapped. The airbag deployed cushioning the blow and protected her face from going through the windshield. Hot marks stung her face where the airbag deployed and broke apart. Pushing its remains aside with her good hand, she was shaken. Other than her broken left arm, Ramirez wasn't badly hurt. She tried to unbuckle her seatbelt and found it jammed. She tried to wriggle out of her seat, but couldn't. The steering column threatened to squeeze the life out of her.

135

After several tries attempting to free herself from the grip of her car's seat, Carlotta knew she was trapped. She panted trying to inhale more air, breathing deeply was difficult. The crushing pain of the steering column squeezed at her midriff and pressed her chest. She looked for her cell phone on the floor but couldn't find it. Darkness had hidden it.

Carlotta heard some rustling in the bushes close to her car. It was so dark she couldn't see very well. What she managed to see was someone she thought could be a man walking toward her holding something in one of his hands. Maybe it was someone who saw what happened and was going to help her. There wasn't anything she could do but wait. In this desolate area, she knew no one would hear her scream for help. About to call out to the man for help, something made her stop.

The figure came nearer to the car and placed a metal container down by the side of the vehicle. The face was hidden beneath a ski mask.

If this guy were going to help me, he'd be running over to see whether I'm all right. But he stopped walking and what is in the can? Oh, God! It's the joker who caused this to happen.

Angry but scared out of her mind, Carlotta demanded, "Who the hell do you think you are? You almost killed me."

Coming closer to the driver's side, the person leaned against the car door. "Almost? It will be corrected momentarily, babe." Carlotta's pursuer reached through the shattered window, brushed away the remaining glass. From a coat pocket out came a gold pin which was fastened to her coat's lapel.

"W-what's this?"

"A little token for you."

The dark form noticed her seat belt held her fast. "I suppose you're not going anywhere, are you?" The pursuer grabbed Carlotta's broken arm and smacked against it the car door. She cried out in agony.

Finding it harder to breathe, her voice became hoarse. She half screamed, half whispered, "Help me. Help me get out of here."

"I don't think so. You're quite expendable. Scream all you want. No one can hear you."

She stared in terror. Carlotta tried to disengage herself from the seatbelt another time. She frantically pushed down on the belt's button attempting to free herself. Carlotta gave it one last try, and she almost released herself from the grip of the belt when she felt a gloved hand push her body to the left preventing her from moving.

"Wha-a-a", she yelled. "What the hell do you think you're doing?"

"You're not getting away so easily."

"Why? Who are you? What do you want from me? Why are you doing this to me? Help me get out of the car. Please. I have money. Take it. It's in my purse. Take anything you want, just help me get out."

"Money isn't what I need. What I *do* need is to get you out of my way."

With Ramirez incapacitated, the phantom was free to continue with the plan.

"Oh, God! W-what are you doing?" Carlotta screamed into the darkness, terrified.

The killer pulled off the ski mask. Carlotta's eyes widened with recognition. "I know you. I saw your picture." Looking up, Carlotta attempted to say the name but failed when a fist knocked her out.

"Sorry about that. Now you're quiet and enjoy the rest of your ride. To hell." The phantom's laughter reverberated in the night as the killer walked away from her and picked up the can. Next, he walked to the passenger side to set it down.

The killer pawed through the Toyota's glove box and rummaged through its contents trying to find her insurance card. Frustrated not finding the card, the killer picked up Carlotta's purse.

What did she do with the file? It must be hidden somewhere. Unless ... unless it's at her home.

The killer searched through her purse on the floor of the passenger side. He found her insurance card displaying her name and address. "Thanks for the calling card to your house, Carlotta Ramirez. I am going there after I tie up some loose ends. Thanks for being so helpful." The killer reached over to the unconscious woman and patted her right arm.

"No one will ever know exactly what happened to you. People will think you became a little sloppy in your driving, is all. You had a nasty, fiery accident. All the better for me."

Carlotta roused and shook her head to focus. She saw through the rearview mirror the contents of the can being poured all over her car. She heard a match struck, then rustling as the killer sped away.

O Dios mio! Get me out of here, please, please, please.

The last thing she felt was an impossibly heavy force weighing her down from an unbearably loud bang. It threatened to tear her body apart. Then, blackness.

Chapter 21

Friday morning

Alison hung her coat on the wire rack behind her desk, when Lakeesha Ellis stopped to speak with her.

"Alison, didja hear?"

"Hear what, Keesh?"

"I'll give you a clue." Ellis cleared her throat and began to sing in a barely recognizable version of the song, "Ding, dong, the bitch is dead."

"What? Huh? What bitch?" She came closer to Lakeesha and asked, "You don't mean Ramirez?"

Lakeesha stopped singing and answered shaking her head quickly up and down.

"Ramirez is dead? No shit."

Lakeesha nodded again, and said, "Oh, it's definitely yeah shit."

"How did you hear about it?"

Lakeesha sang an out-of-tune, "I heard it through the grapevine," while rolling her eyes and jutting out her chin towards Pat Owens's opened office door.

"Holy shit. I only wanted Ramirez out of my life, not hers."

Pat Owens stood at the opened door of her office and called out to Alison. "Alison, may I see you privately for a moment, please? We need to talk."

PINNED FOR DEATH

Lakeesha squeezed Alison's shoulder then walked toward her own cubicle. Alison followed Owens into her office.

When she entered the small office and stopped at the door, Pat said, "Please come in, sit down and close the door."

Alison's heart sank. She obeyed. "Lakeesha told me Carlotta is dead. Is it true?"

"Unfortunately, it is. It's what I wanted to speak with you about."

"My, God. What the hell happened to her?" Alison placed a hand to her mouth.

"Alison, Carlotta had a terrible accident last night."

"What kind of accident? She told me she'd be visiting her sister's and coming home late. She told me not to wait for her, go to work and begin on the case we were working on. She wasn't coming in today."

"Apparently she lost control of her car on a secondary road off the Route 1 bypass, and she landed in a ditch. Her car exploded with her trapped inside."

"Oh, my God. What? How? You're kidding me, right?"

"No, I'm not. Carlotta was killed instantly in the fiery crash."

"How did you find out?"

"Carlotta's sister, Oceola Murphy, became very worried when she didn't arrive at her home for their weekly dinner. Oceola tried Carlotta's cell phone which went straight to voicemail. It was very strange since Carlotta never turned her cell off in case of family emergencies. When Carlotta hadn't been reached, Oceola called 911, and the dispatcher took down the information. The route Carlotta always took to her home had been checked and, unfortunately, Carlotta's wrecked, burned-out car was found in a ditch off a lonely road."

Icy fingers of guilt wrapped around Alison's throat threatening to choke her. She couldn't find her voice for what seemed like forever.

After some moments and finally being able to talk, Alison asked, "H-how did this happen to her? I don't believe this. I can't believe it. No, no. It's a mistake. It has to be. I know Carlotta is such a careful driver. This is so unreal. No, no. This isn't happening. It can't be true—"

Sobs racked Alison's body as she placed her head down on folded arms onto Owens's desk.

Did she die because of me? Is this a coincidence, or was she murdered? If she was murdered, then it's all my fault. Ramirez dug deeper into this Costello mess, and she's dead. All because of me.

"I'm so sorry, Alison. I know it's hard to believe about Carlotta," Pat Owens rose from her desk, walked around to Alison and placed a reassuring hand on the young girl's shoulder.

Lifting her head from the desk, Alison sniffed while shaking her head in agreement.

Pat offered Alison a tissue from a box. The young girl took one. The older woman continued, "Her sister told me when final arrangements are made she'll contact me. After conclusive information is obtained from the autopsy, Carlotta's funeral will be held probably sometime next week. I am thinking about a memorial service, too, for those not able to attend Carlotta's funeral. Alison, are you okay?"

Alison just nodded at first, but then shook her head from side to side, sniffed, then blew her nose into the tissue.

"Alison, we need to pick up where she left off. I handed over the Costello case to one of our junior partners. I called Regina's family early this morning and told them what happened to Ms. Ramirez. When I spoke with Mrs. Costello, she told me she wants the firm to finish the case for their son, and now," she sighed, "their daughter. Will you help them out on this?"

"Okay. But, Pat, who will be taking up the case?"

"Oh, yes, it's Thomas Humphrey. You will be reporting to him."

Alison felt she had been sucker punched when she heard new her assignment.

"B-but how—"

"Tom asked for the case since his work load is light, and of course, I gave it to him."

"Of course." Alison gulped and tried to explain, "Pat, I can't do this. I can't work with—"

"You will have to put all of your sensitivities aside. I understand you have a right to be emotional over what has happened, but you certainly can't break down about these cases. They need to be dealt with and now. I don't want to hear any gripes from you. You are an intelligent, young woman, and this is part of your responsibilities. Since you were assigned to the Costello case at the outset, you must continue and follow it through to its completion. This is an order."

"B-but, you don't understand. I … just … can't … do … it … with … him." Alison's words fell on deaf ears. She had to resign herself to the fact she would be working with Thomas Humphrey whose incredibly horrible performance on stage kept replaying in her mind.

***

In the break room, Alison harshly whispered, "Oh, God, I'm so dead meat. Keesh, what the hell do I do now? If Humphrey gets wind of what my videoing him, I'm history."

"Allie, girl, he sure won't hear it from me. It's a guarantee."

"Oh, I know you wouldn't do it, but what if somebody else was at the Back Draught? Just my stupid luck someone saw me taking Jiggle Hips's video. I just know it. Oh, God. I'm in major deep shit now."

"Keep your cool, girlfriend. If anyone did see you take the video, they might give you a medal for exposin' bad karaoke singin'."

"Yeah, right. I should be so lucky. But, anyway," Alison sighed, "I gotta get my stuff together in my work station and report to He Who Should Not Be Named."

Lakeesha rolled her eyes. "Good luck."

"Thanks. I'll really need it this time."

***

After gathering up the needed materials on the Costello case, Alison made her way to Humphrey's office. She knocked on the lawyer's door when it opened to let a client out of the room. Humphrey ushered her in so he could discuss the Costello case with her. They exchanged introductions while Humphrey showed Alison to a chair in his office.

"W-what do we do first?" Alison asked, a bit intimidated by the man, she sat in the offered chair attempting to compose herself.

"Well, I'll need to go through the Costello case to familiarize myself with it and see what has transpired between Marco's trial and now. I'll handle the paperwork exonerating Marco Costello's name. From what happened to Regina, Marco certainly was not Jeannette Turner's killer. This should relieve their parents."

"Are you kidding me?"

Her statement made Humphrey stop in his tracks, saying, "Alison, what are you talking about? Regina's unfortunate death proves Marco didn't kill Jeannette Turner. This new murder exonerates him completely."

"You are totally clueless. Not to diss you, but you haven't heard the latest."

"Don't tell me you actually think Marco put someone up to kill his sister, when he's in a coma?"

"No, no way. Marco's not in a coma. He's out."

"What?"

"He's not in jail. Which means he still could've killed Jeannette Turner, and maybe someone *else* Marco knew could've killed Regina. Carlotta and I were working on the idea."

"Who could it have been?"

"Okay. I guess it's all right I tell you this, since Carlotta's a permanent resident of the Great Beyond. The last thing she and I were discussing about the Costello case was Marco knew a Richard Parker through the insurance company they worked for. It's how Marco Costello and Jeannette Turner hooked up. Through this Richard Parker guy, I mean.

PINNED FOR DEATH

We were thinking, Carlotta and me, maybe Marco and Richard *both* killed Jeannette, but Richard went free while Marco took the rap."

"If it's true, then Richard Parker sounds like more of a bastard than Marco's friend."

"Yeah, more like Marco's worst frenemy."

"Excuse me?"

"You know, frenemy. Your friend, who really does stuff against you like an enemy would. You know. Your frenemy."

"Oh, like someone who stabs you in the back," Humphrey offered.

"Yeah," she rolled her eyes. "You got it."

"You know, Alison? I like you, and I like your way of thinking. We're going to make a great team, you and I. Yes, we will."

She looked straight at him. *Not after what I have on you, Mister Jiggle Hips.* Then smiled with a toothy grin. "Oh, sure. A great team."

"Well, Regina's parents must be aware their son is on the loose."

"Oh, I'm sure they're very aware."

Humphrey looked at Alison warily and asked, "But you're still convinced Marco could've killed Jeannette, aren't you?"

"Yep. The noose is still tight around the guy's neck. And about Richard Parker … " she trailed off.

"Look, as far as we know, Richard Parker had nothing to do with Jeannette's or Regina's death.

147

There's no evidence linking Richard to either murder. Until there is, whoever killed Regina is still out there, and it's up to the police to find it out. I will be working with the police and you will report to me. Don't work on your own. Only through me. Clear?"

"Uh, huh. I-I mean y-yes sir. No involvement with any police investigation unless you say so. Then I guess you'll be talking to Regina's parents about how to deal with the Marco problem." Alison answered trying to remain calm in Humphrey's presence.

"I see you're still not completely convinced about Marco's innocence."

"And I really won't be until the Turner case is positively, absolutely solved, which I don't think it ever really was."

"I see."

"Yeah, you can see all you want. But my gut feeling says something else. And, it will all come out, sir."

"Alison, you don't need to be so formal. You may call me Tom."

"Okay, uh, Tom." Changing the subject, she said, "Isn't it terrible what happened to Carlotta?"

His eyebrows raised. "Yes. It certainly is quite a shock. Carlotta was a good lawyer. She'll certainly be missed around here," Humphrey said as he rose from his seat and came around his desk over to Alison and sat down in a chair next to her. The way in which he loped around the furniture brought back a memory of his sleazy stage performance making her begin to laugh. She caught herself while biting her lip and covering her mouth to stifle the urge to giggle in front of him.

"Yeah, she will," Alison answered. She dabbed at her eyes with the used tissue she still had as though she were trying to stop tears from falling and avoided meeting his eyes. She sighed deeply trying to control the urge to break out in laughter.

"Alison. Alison. Control yourself," Humphrey said with concern. He looked directly at her and added, "One thing you'll need to learn about handling criminal cases, murder cases especially. You must disassociate yourself from the details. No matter how close to the facts you happen to be involved with. If you don't remember that, then you're doomed to fall apart on every case you'll be assigned. I know this is difficult for you."

"Y-yes it is difficult, but I'll do it. Thanks, Tom. I'm sorry," she bit her lip.

"No need to apologize. You're too close to this one. But nevertheless, Alison, I do need you."

Humphrey came close to Alison. "You're quite adept with a smart phone."

"W-what?" Alison almost choked on the word and her face paled.

"I only mean you know how to use the device's different features. Your phone could be quite useful for doing some research."

Alison recovered with a deep exhale. "Research? Oh, oh, yeah. Research. Of course."

Humphrey stared at her. "Yes, you know. Use the phone's apps to help you get what you want. Like taking notes. Or, videos."

Shit! He knows. How? Don't know. That's the real reason he took the case. I can't let on. I'll play it cool and see what happens.

Alison stared back at him. "Tom, where do I start? I-I feel so inadequate researching details on cases, especially this one. I'm so new at this. I don't want to screw up anything, especially since it involves someone I was working so closely with."

"Alison, this is your first murder case, isn't it?"

"Yuh, huh."

"Well, this is the big time. I don't tolerate lame excuses or laziness. I'll show you what needs to be done. And as long as you do what I tell you, we'll get along just fine."

"Y-yes, sir, I-I mean, Tom. It's so weird."

"Weird?"

"Well, you know, Carlotta getting killed in a car crash. A fiery one, no less. Aren't you a little creeped out?"

"Why?"

"'Cause of her dying the way she did. I-I mean Carlotta was working on the Costello case, and now she's *dead*, and I was thinking I would certainly be especially careful if I were the next lawyer taking on the Costello case. Something strange could happen to me, too, if I—"

Humphrey interrupted her. "Let's see what we have here. You take the file. I want copies of all the materials Carlotta had in it. Then I can write a sketch of what we already know about Marco Costello. You know, have a timeline of his movements on that fateful day."

"Like what?"

"Focus, Alison. You must stay with me on this case."

"Oh, you won't believe how focused I can be." She rolled her eyes again.

"Okay, then. Now, where was I? Oh, yes. Like where Marco was at the time of the murder. What he was doing. Maybe something else significant will turn up. We'll need to find out who he was with at the time of the murder, too. If he was seeing someone other than Jeannette Turner, for instance. I'm sure Carlotta made up a list of people Marco had been seen with a couple of weeks before Jeannette's murder. Using the information you can determine what facts begin to fall into place. Try to discover any clues Carlotta might have missed."

"Where do I go to get this information, Tom? I feel at such a loss."

"You'll need to go to the Roundhouse. For any other details concerning the Turner case, you'll need to see the medical examiner."

"Uh, the police station? And the morgue?"

"Is there a problem?"

"Uh, yeah. The morgue thing I can do, maybe, but I can't do the police department thing."

"And why not? Are you in some sort of trouble?"

"No, uh—"

"Alison, what is it?" Humphrey urged. "I need to know."

She put up her hands in front of her face while saying, "I know, I know, I know. It's all coming out anyway, so I might as well tell you. Tom, Carlotta was helping me out with this, and I think this is why she was killed. I suspect Carlotta was murdered. I'm sure of it."

Humphrey moved so close to her, his face nearly touched Alison's. "Murdered? By whom?"

Startled by his abrupt movement toward her, she jumped back in her seat for fear of being consumed by his mint breath, she stammered, "W-whoever k-killed Jeannette Turner and-and Regina Costello."

"So why can't you go to the police about this?"

"B-because I was threatened by the killer."

"And what were you threatened with?" He noticed the effect of coming too close to her and moved back at a more appropriate distance.

Still alarmed, she rattled off the events as she remembered them.

"Alison. Why didn't you say something to Pat Owens?"

"B-because Carlotta … Carlotta was going to take care of business, and-and she thought the fewer people knew, the better for everyone, I guess, s-so she could straighten it all out. I-I've been living at her house."

"Living at Carlotta's?"

Alison nodded.

"Do you still have the threatening note?"

"No. We dropped it off at the Roundhouse. I made a copy and gave it to Carlotta. She has, uh had, it. I-I don't know what she did with it, but if it's in the Costello file, I can give it to you."

"Okay," Humphrey said slowly, "I can see it later. But, you'll still need to go to the police. Are you up to it? You know, Alison, killers who use notes to intimidate people, rarely go through with their threats."

"Oh, yeah? But look what happened to Carlotta."

"Don't you think it's more likely Carlotta could just have had a nasty accident?"

"No, I don't think so. Carlotta was a careful driver. You know yourself she's always is, uh, always *was*, in control of everything she did. Even me."

"Excuse me?"

"Sorry, Tom. Forget what I said."

"People have accidents all the time."

"I'm not trying to dodge the work. How do you expect me to do all the research in one day?"

"You won't. This case will take some time to organize all the facts. But you will have a lot of people to help you out. Like the coroner, the police."

"Oh, yes. Officer Hedley." Alison interrupted.

"You know someone in the police department?" He came close to Alison again.

"Uh, yeah. He's the officer I spoke to on the night of my finding Regina Costello's body. I can get in touch with him, because he gave me his card," Alison answered calmly.

"Okay, then. What's his name again?" he said ready to write the officer's name on a note pad.

"Officer Michael Hedley."

He finished scribbling on the pad and looked at her. "Alison, you have all the ammunition you need to assist me in resolving the puzzles in this case. I'm glad you decided to do this. Ms. Costello's family will be very grateful, I'm sure."

"Yeah. Hopefully if I can find some answers about the Costello case, it'll solve Ramirez's murder, too," she across at Humphrey's stern face when she said "murder" and added, "It's just such a waste. People dying so young. Well, at least in Jeannette's and Regina's cases. Carlotta was an old fogey."

"Alison. That was uncalled for. Carlotta was an upstanding integral part of this firm. She was only in her fifties."

"Sorry. But, you know, at least Carlotta had a chance to have a life and do something with it. She became somebody. A lawyer. But when I read over the notes I found on Jeannette Turner, you know, about the Costello case, I thought, 'Gee, she was only twenty-four years old'. And her life stopped in its tracks before she ever had a chance to live. It's all I meant."

"Hm-m. The statement you made would probably make poor Carlotta turn over in her grave, if she already had been buried."

Alison stared upward as if in prayer.

"Well, I guess that's it for now. Do you understand what you are to do?"

Alison answered with a quick nod of her head.

Humphrey added, "Okay, and if you can find the copy of the note sent to you, it would be very helpful to keep everything together in one place. Very helpful indeed."

"Okay, Tom, I'll do my best. If it's not in the file, it could be in her office. If not there, the police have the original. But, anyway, I'll get permission to use a spare key from Pat."

With a sigh of relief she didn't give herself away, Alison walked out of Humphrey's office determined to discover all she could.

Does he really know about the video? Can't be sure.

Alison made the requested copies for Humphrey and dropped the original and one copy off at his office. She kept the other copy. A copy of the nasty note wasn't in with the files. Alison got the spare key to Ramirez's office and entered. Jeannette Turner's and Regina Costello's files were there on the desk.

Alison determined there could be clues scattered throughout the files. Her plan was to thoroughly read through Ramirez's copies of Jeannette Turner's file, Marco Costello's and Regina's, compare all three cases, to see what the notes Ramirez took show. Who knew? Maybe there would be something to connect all three cases.

The note.

Where would Carlotta have kept it? It must be around here somewhere.

Alison rummaged through the desk and found nothing. Then, she noticed something sticking out from under the dead woman's laptop and pulled it out. Sure enough, it was the copy encased in a baggie. The young girl picked up the baggie and studied it.

PINNED FOR DEATH

Did you want me to find it? I'll never know for sure, but I think you were trying to protect me. Maybe you really did *like me.*

Alison sighed as a tear dropped from her eye. She brushed the tear away and read through Ramirez's notes carefully in order to compare the cases. She needed to see what matched and what didn't. Alison readied herself to make another trip to the Roundhouse.

After giving the note to Humphrey, she began her trip. Alison made a mental list of the facts she had studied concerning the Jeannette Turner and Regina Costello cases.

1. Jeannette and Regina were stabbed with a knife.
2. Neither victim had any ID on their bodies when they were found.
3. They were murdered two years apart.
4. Each woman had the same style gold pin on their lapel with their respective initials.

With the mental list of the facts firmed etched in her mind, Alison knew what questions to ask the police and what other clues to look for. It was time to see Officer Hedley. A blush caressed her cheeks along with a flutter in her stomach.

***

By chance, the man spotted Alison about a block in front of him. He followed, trying to keep up with her

BEVERLY ANN MEYERS

fast pace. The biting wind and his injured leg held him back. He knew where she was headed.

Alison. You didn't listen to my warning. You don't realize what danger you are getting yourself into.

Chapter 22

Alison placed her valise on the floor of the reception area at the Roundhouse police station. "Hi. I came to see Officer Michael Hedley."

The receptionist loomed over the huge desk. "And you are?"

"Oh, yeah. Sorry. My name is Alison Caldwell. I'm a paralegal from the law firm of Dunbar, Engels, and Quinn. I called him earlier today, and he said I could come anytime this afternoon to see him at the station. We met a couple of weeks ago. I-I mean him and me met a couple of weeks ago during a case." *Steady, Allie. Remember professionalism.*

The woman recording the information gave Alison a distrustful stare over her bifocals.

"Oh, oh! No, no, no. It's nothing like that," Alison waved both hands in the air, sensing the woman's suspicions. Alison stammered, blushing and sweating profusely, "This is purely professional. I'm doing some research on a case I have been assigned and I need to—" The poor girl hesitated between words as she explained, "tell Officer Hedley, what I've discovered and to help me out further on, on this investigation." More quickly, she continued, "And so, I'd like to know if he is still free to see me and all."

"I see. Wait here please. I'll call his extension to see if Officer Hedley is available."

That went well. Not. Nothing like falling all over myself while trying to act like I know exactly what I'm doing. Why do I suddenly have foot-in-mouth disease when I mention Mick's name, or even think about him? Oh, God! Ms. Bulldozer won't allow me to see him. I know it. I blew it big time.

While Alison's posture slumped, she agonized over her lousy impression with the receptionist at the front desk. A shadow came across the floor and a familiar voice asked, "Well, Miss Caldwell, are you ready to get to work?"

She turned slowly around and faced Hedley. She looked up into those gentle, blue eyes smiling back at her and answered, "I-I guess I'm as ready as I'll ever be."

"Why don't we discuss things over a cup of coffee? We can use one of the empty interrogation rooms upstairs. It's private. Nobody should hear what we're discussing, especially since this is a sensitive case. Tell me what you would like to have, and I'll have it fixed up for you. What do you say?"

Her apprehension still lingering, she gulped an answer, "Th-that would be really cool. I-I mean, sure. I'd love having a coffee of cup with you."

His eyes crinkled as he laughed.

"D-did I say something wrong?"

"No. Nothing at all. You couldn't say or do anything wrong if you tried. Let's go," Hedley held

160

out his hand leading Alison toward the elevator to the second floor.

Ms. Bulldozer Receptionist scowled as her eyes followed the couple.

Alison glad to be inside the warmth of the Roundhouse and free from December's biting cold. Its stinging mark remained on her rosy cheeks. Inside the elevator, she felt an immediate rush of heat on her face and the quickening of her heart as she stood beside Hedley in the elevator.

The door opened and they chatted walking to one of the empty rooms.

"Here we are," Hedley held the door open for her.

"Thank you."

Before entering, Alison was eager to tell Hedley about the recent developments in the case she was working on, but he quickly brought up a finger to his lips and made a shushing sound signaling her to be quiet. She obeyed.

When the door to the room was closed, Alison told Hedley about being assigned to the Marco Costello case and to discover who murdered his sister, Regina.

"That's a big step for a young, fresh-from-school paralegal."

"I know." With a deep breath, she added. "Well, it's become a personal thing, too, because I worked under Carlotta Ramirez. She was the lawyer I told you about who handled the reopening of the Costello case."

"Before we get started, how about a coffee to take the chill off?"

"That'd be sweet. Real sweet."

"How do you like your coffee?"

"Milk and two sugars, please."

"I think it can be arranged with no trouble at all. Here, let me take your coat so you'll be more comfortable. I'll be right back with our orders."

As he helped her with her coat, Alison felt a pleasant tingle throughout her body. "Thanks." A blossoming smile spread across her face.

It only took a few minutes for Hedley to return with their coffees.

When they were settled in their seats, Hedley said, "Now let's get down to business. Tell me what you know about the Costello case."

Taking a quick sip, Alison said, "Well, let's see."

With a warm blush rising on her face and a quiver in her stomach, she looked at her notes to avoid staring at his amused face. "Before I tell you, any word on finding Marco Costello?"

"No. He hasn't turned up. Officer Peterson and I went to the Costello home. Of course they were shocked to learn their son wasn't in prison but is out on the street. At least, it's how they appeared."

Alison realized what Hedley told her. "You believe they're hiding something?" She raised her brows. "Maybe even hiding him?"

Hedley spread out his arms. "Could be. We came with a warrant to search the house. We didn't find any evidence Costello was living there."

"Did they give you an address where he lived before he was arrested?"

He rested his arms on the table. "Yes. We checked it out, and of course, someone else is living at his old address."

Alison frowned. "Of course. Then, where is he? Where has Marco been living? On the street? With Richard Parker? Someone else?"

"Who's Richard Parker?"

"Oh. Then, you don't know. Carlotta found out from his coworkers Marco Costello was seeing a Richard Parker, who also attended the insurance convention."

"Costello was seeing a Richard Parker? Seeing like in having an affair?"

Alison arched her eyebrows. "Well, sort of. Yeah. We both were wondering, uh, you know, Carlotta and me, if Richard Parker could have had anything to do with *her* murder. I-I mean Regina's. And who wrote me the note? Richard? Was he the one who saw me tell you what happened on Ramstead Street? Everything seems to point to Richard Parker.

If so, then Marco was innocent of Jeannette's murder, like Regina and her family believed him to be."

Hedley leaned forward and rested his chin on his hands. "You suspect Parker to be the murderer?"

"Well, I guess. He's the only one I can think of. Of course, it could be someone else too. But the way I see it, Richard seems to be the one."

"What about Regina's fiancé? Or, Costello's parents?"

"Nah. Regina told us, Eddie Sandroni, the fiancé didn't know Jeannette Turner. He's her dad's partner in the mercantile business. As for Mom and Dad Costello? They're too old. And, anyway, it sounds too cliché."

Hedley smiled at the explanation. "Everything about the note has been documented?"

"Yeah. I'm still on the case to clear it up, and I came with all the notes I've been taking."

Hedley scanned Alison's legal pad. "I see. You've kept good notes and documented all the details."

"Thanks. It's what I told Ramirez before she was killed."

"Wait a minute. Carlotta Ramirez is dead?"

"Uh, yeah. She was going to see her sister, and she was killed in a terrible fiery car crash last night. I found out about it this morning."

"It's the case Dom's working on."

"Dom? Who's Dom?"

"He's a coroner friend of mine. We go back a few years."

"Oh."

Hedley took a sip of his coffee. "But back to you on this case. What did you say to Ramirez?"

"I told her I thought the *real* murderer is Richard Parker. She seemed to agree with me. She found out through some people who were at the insurance convention Richard Parker and Marco Costello knew each other real-ly well. Too well." Alison gave Hedley a knowing look. "I thought maybe both guys confronted Jeannette to tell her the engagement was off. She got pissed off. First about finding out Marco was gay and, second her fiancé cheated on her with Richard."

Alison looked down at her notes, then at Hedley, and continued. "Maybe there was a fight. A terrible fight and Jeannette was killed. But I also told Carlotta I wasn't completely convinced of Marco's innocence. She could've been killed by accident by either guy, or both. They got together, and left her body in a dumpster. By the time she had been found, her body was so badly decomposed no one could ID her until much later."

Alison picked up her Styrofoam coffee cup, and held it. "Does it sound plausible? Could it have happened that way? They had no intention of killing Jeannette, but it was an unfortunate accident? Both of them needed to cover the whole thing up 'cause of ...

well, embarrassment. You know. Marco and/or Richard couldn't come out about being gay. Some families can't understand about the gay thing." The girl took a sip of the beverage then put down the cup.

"I don't know. It could've happened that way. But, then, why was the sister killed?"

Alison scratched her head. "Well, maybe Regina found out about them, and she threatened to tell the parents. You think?"

"It's possible."

"And Richard felt threatened at work. From what Carlotta found out, he's head of sales in the insurance company. The company could be homo-freakin'-phobic."

Hedley sat back in his chair. "Hm-m. Never thought of it that way."

"We should see Richard Parker and ask *him* what really happened. Don't you think?"

"Alison, it's really police business, and could prove to be dangerous for you to be asking Richard Parker any questions."

"But couldn't I go along? I'll be asking him general things. I mean you'll be there with me, and I won't be interfering with anything. I do need to finish work on the Costello case, 'cause Regina's family is depending on the firm finding out why she was killed, too. And, maybe clearing things up about Marco one way or the other."

Sternly, Hedley instructed. "Stay close to home. When we find out anything substantial, I'll get back to you. Got it?"

"Got it," Alison replied dejected, realizing she wasn't going to learn anything first hand. "Oh, and speaking of home?"

"Yes?"

"I better give you the address where I'm staying now."

"Oh, when did you move?"

"Well-l, it's like this. I really didn't move, I, uh, have been staying at Carlotta's since the Monday night after Regina's murder." She winced as she said, "When I had received the threatening letter from the killer, I told Carlotta about it, the letter, I mean, and she said I should stay with her. I live in an apartment behind her house."

"She did that for you?"

"Yeah. She thought it would be safer for me to live there until this whole mess was settled. And now that she's dead, I really don't know what to do. Should I stay there? Is *her* place safe now? Or what?"

Hedley raised an eyebrow. "Have you received any more threatening notes?"

"No."

"Do you feel safe at Carlotta's?"

She shrugged. "Uh, yeah. I guess so."

"Well, under these circumstances, I think it should be safe for you to stay there until things are solved with these cases. When everything is resolved, then you'll need to return to your own place, do you understand?"

"Uh, huh."

Hedley waved a finger at Alison. "Okay. I'm going to call Frank Peterson on this. You're returning to work. I don't want anything bad happening to you. C'mon, let's go."

"Now?"

"Now. Let me see if Frank's in. He could be out on another case."

Hedley punched in Peterson's extension on his cell phone. After the third ring, Peterson answered.

"Peterson here."

"Frank, we need to see a possible crime suspect. Get the addresses for Richard Parker's residence and his work. The info is in the case files for Marco Costello. Come by my work station when you return. Then, we can pay Parker a little visit. If he's not at work, we'll search his place."

"The Costello case? It's still ongoin'?"

"Yeah. Costello's sister turned up dead last week and this Richard Parker could be a suspect. I'll fill you in when I see you."

"See you in a few, Mick," Frank hung up with a click.

PINNED FOR DEATH

To Alison, "Okay, that's settled. You return to work."

"Yes, sir," Alison answered.

Chapter 23

Dom Vitalli scrutinized the charred remains of the woman's body. According to the victim's broken watch, time of the accident was around 6:30 on Wednesday evening, December 1. He needed to carefully peel some debris of the airbag from what remained of the victim's face. The bag's cushion protected the woman's head from the impact the car sustained, but not from the flames. Parts of the pantsuit the woman wore were melted into her flesh. From his rudimentary examination, he could determine there were extensive internal injuries.

The accident appeared very suspicious to the ME. At the scene, there wasn't a steep embankment. The woman's car wound up at the bottom of a slight hill. By rights, the victim should have walked away.

But a fiery crash? No! This smells bad. Really bad.

From all accounts, the car could have been pushed from behind. Forensics took paint residue from another vehicle on the trunk of the Toyota. Also, there was the faint odor of gasoline. Was gasoline the cause of the explosion? All very suspicious.

Vitalli stared at the scorched remains of Carlotta Ramirez's face. Her eye sockets. Those staring, empty eye sockets peering at him as if they were attempting to communicate with him. The mouth was frozen in a scream.

PINNED FOR DEATH

"What are you trying to tell me, Carlotta? Please tell me, my dear," Vitalli wanted to know. By rights the woman should only have suffered bruises on her head and chest, at most her left arm was fractured, and yet her lifeless form told him a gruesome story.

"Yo, Dom! Are you in here?" Detective Jackson called.

Broken from his concentration on the body, Vitalli answered, "Yeah, yeah, Trev. I'm here. Come on back."

"We found something interesting back at the accident scene."

"What is it? What have you got for me?"

"This was no accident. The poor broad was murdered. We found tire tracks all around the crime scene," Jackson laid out some photos on another exam table. "A rookie stomped around in the grass near the accident site and practically fell in one of 'em."

"Then the Ramirez woman didn't succumb to the accident."

"Nope. That's what it looks like to me."

Vitally slapped his gloved hand on the edge of the exam table. "Son-of-a-bitch. I see. Yes, I see exactly what happened. The killer initiated the accident, found the vic trapped in her car," Vitalli shook his index finger at Jackson. "And Ramirez's body along with her Toyota was burned to deliberately cover it up. Why? Why was it necessary to destroy the body?" he asked the other man.

"I'll tell ya what I think. How's this. Regina Costello had asked Carlotta Ramirez to reopen her brother's case. The case where Marco Costello was convicted of killing Jeannette Turner," Jackson answered Vitalli's question. "And *that's* why the Regina Costello case seemed so familiar to me. Think about it, Dom. The Jeannette Turner, Regina Costello *and* Carlotta Ramirez deaths are all connected."

"Yes. But how?"

"Did you check Ramirez' body thoroughly?"

"Sure. What was left of it."

"Did you check her clothes?"

Vitalli picked up the evidence bag containing charred remains of the dead woman's clothing. "Oh, I know exactly what you're thinking. The pin. Let me see. If there's a gold initial pin in here, then that's the connection."

After carefully removing items in the bag and placing them on the adjacent exam table, Vitalli found a bit of metal attached to a burned piece of coat.

"Dom, let me do the honors so's I can take look under the microscope to be sure."

"Sounds like a plan."

Jackson adjusted the instrument and peered through the lens. "Well, looky here. We got us a connection. Now, you take a look, and tell me exactly what you see."

Jackson moved away enabling Vitalli to inspect the detective's findings. The coroner squinted into the instrument's lens. "Sonofabitch! I can make out part of a 'C' with what looks like a shaft. You're right. There it is. The microscope doesn't lie."

"What's botherin' you about this case, my friend?"

Vitalli pushed the microscope aside. "We know the how, but we still don't know the why."

"In all the cases I've ever worked on, the killer manages to goof somehow. The pin is his calling card. But the tire tracks are his goof. It don't take long ta find out who the vehicle belongs to. When we do, he'll be in really deep shit."

"But if the SUV was stolen, the killer's still in the clear."

"If so, he'll goof up again. It's only a matter of time." Jackson placed one hand over his heart. "They always do. It's my job to figger it out."

"This could give you a coupla clues. About a week ago, Carlotta came to me about the Marco Costello case. She asked me if I did the autopsy on Jeannette Turner. I said I did. She wanted to know every detail about it, because Regina, his sister, came into her office with new evidence proving Marco was nowhere near Philly when the murder happened. He was in Baltimore."

"But Baltimore is just two hours away, Dom. He could've made some excuse to return to Philly, kill Jeannette, dump her body in the trash, and return to Baltimore within, let's see, give or take five hours. Plenty of time."

"Five hours? Then Marco had to be damn certain everything went according to plan. One slip up, even a traffic jam, for instance, and his plot would be all over. If he didn't return to the conference in time, then—"

"Yeah, but ya see," Jackson interjected, "There's somethin' about Marco you don't know. And I found out about it only a little while ago. This insurance conference Marco went to?"

"Yes? So?"

"Oh, it was a conference all right. But not dealing mainly with insurance."

"Then—"

Jackson interrupted Vitalli, "Marco had another life. He was gay."

"Nah. It's a fact he was to marry Jeannette Turner. He and Jeannette probably had a fight, and he killed her. And that was that."

"Marco was runnin' AC/DC. Apparently from one of the witnesses, who swears he saw Marco at the conference. Marco confided in the guy and went to tell Jeannette it was over. Tell her about this other guy he was seein'. Dom, Marco was cheatin' on Jeannette with another *guy*."

174

PINNED FOR DEATH

Vitalli's eyes widened. "Woo hoo! Do you know the name of this guy?"

"Yep. Read this little tidbit," Jackson shoved the open file under Vitalli's nose.

Vitalli read aloud from the sheet of paper, "Richard Parker? Marco Costello had an affair with Richard Parker? You think Marco killed Jeannette because of Parker?"

Jackson snapped the file closed. "Sure does look that way. See ya. I hafta pay Richard Parker a little visit."

Chapter 24

Jackson wasted no time. He took out his badge and showed it to the receptionist as he approached her desk at Wentworth Insurance, Inc. "Ma'am, I'm Detective Trevor Jackson, Philadelphia Police, and I'd like to see Richard Parker on official business." Taken completely off guard, the woman peered up at him, and stammered, "W-whatever for, officer?"

"Is he at work today, Miss, uh—"

"It's *Mrs*. Braeburn," she smiled at him. "Please wait over there." She motioned for Jackson to sit on a couch far from her desk. He refused to move away. Braeburn shook her head. "I'll check to see if he's in his office, detective."

She called Parker's extension, waited until she heard his voice on the phone. "Richard, there's a detective here to see you."

She paused while Parker answered.

"No. He didn't say what he wanted. Only he wished to see you. Shall I send him up to your office?"

Not waiting for a reply, Jackson read the directory on the wall to the side of Braeburn's desk, and he raced to catch an elevator to the second floor. The doors closed in front of him.

Braeburn stabbed the phone's keypad for security to go to Parker's office.

PINNED FOR DEATH

The elevator's doors opened and Jackson exited. He read the office numbers on the wall and turned right. He followed the hallway around until he found the door to Room 231 closed with Parker's name printed on it in bold black letters.

He knocked on the office door while calling out, "Richard Parker? This is Detective Trevor Jackson, Philadelphia P. D. I'd like to ask you some questions. Open the door."

There was no response.

Again, with more force in his voice, "Richard Parker, open this door. I need to ask you some questions about—"

Jackson heard some rumbling behind the door. He took his gun out of its holster and holding it in his hand as he said, "You have a choice. Either open up, or I break down the door."

Still no response. This time all was quiet within the office. As Jackson went to ram the door open with his foot, a security guard came running towards Room 231.

The guard shouted at Jackson. "Mrs. Braeburn sent me up to help. What's happnin'?"

Jackson answered, "I need to speak with Richard Parker. I was told he's here today, and need to ask him some questions about a criminal case."

The guard knocked on the door. Getting no response, he called out, "Richard Parker? This is security. I need to speak with you."

Again, no answer.

Hillary Wentworth came out of her office and saw the commotion. She stepped forward demanded an explanation, "What's going on here?"

"I need to question Richard Parker. It's police business," Jackson informed her. "And who might you be?"

"I'm Hillary Wentworth, president of this company." She continued, "Well, we all know Richard Parker. He's an outstanding member of our sales team, with an excellent record."

"I need to ask him a few questions. Could you please open his door so I may speak with him? He's not answerin'."

"After I see your credentials."

"Of course." Jackson showed Wentworth his badge.

"Let me open the door. I have a master key," which the woman did without hesitation.

When the door opened she called out to Parker, but found the office empty.

Jackson and the security guard went over to the open window and looked right and left. There was no sign of Richard Parker. The guard offered, "M-m-m. Sumpin' up with him."

"Parker was here, but apparently he had some other important business to attend to," Jackson sneered at Wentworth. "I'll need his home address." Looking directly at the president, he held his hand out

PINNED FOR DEATH

in front of him, "If you'll be so kind, Ms. Wentworth."

"Allow me to get his home address for you, detective. I'll be a few minutes. Wait right here."

"Believe me, I ain't movin'," Jackson glared at the crowd of people milling around Parker's office. Wentworth returned with Parker's address scribbled on a note pad. "Here you are," Wentworth handed Jackson the requested information.

"Thanks for your assistance, Ms. Wentworth. I hope for your sake Parker doesn't decide to leave the country. It could be on your conscience."

Wentworth glared at Jackson.

After looking over and pocketing Parker's home address, Jackson turned and left.

Chapter 25

"You have Parker's address?" asked Mick Hedley, as he pulled the squad car out of the station's parking lot.

"Yup. Old Jackson called it in to the station. I got it right here. We need to get to the 300 block of South 15th Street."

"Sounds like it's near the Touraine. Just a short hop away."

"Well, the exact address is 324 South 15th," Peterson told him.

"Yeah, it's a Trinity. There are all Trinities down there. One of my uncles, Uncle Paddy, owned a Trinity in South Philly. He used to call it his Father, Son, and Oh-my-achin' Feet house, because each floor had only one or two rooms."

"Okay. Here is Parker's place. Uh, oh! What's all this?" Peterson pulled the squad car to a hasty stop.

"Looks like we got company of the official kind," Hedley answered as both officers got out of the car.

Hedley immediately walked up to a patrolwoman standing around the cordoned-off area at the far end of 15th Street. Two squad cars were blocking on-coming traffic and a lone patrolman was detouring cars from traveling on the street.

"What's going on, here, officer?"

PINNED FOR DEATH

"There was a homicide. A man. You're Officer Hedley? And this is your partner with you? Officer Peterson? Okay. Detective Jackson wants both of you on the premises on the second floor ASAP."

Hedley and Peterson entered the house bounding up the staircase to the second-floor bedroom crawled with police. There, on the floor, was the body of a man on his side. He wore a three-piece business suit. A pool of blood spread out from beneath his form. Something gleamed between his first finger and thumb. The forensics team snapped pictures of the crime scene. The room was a flurry of activity as it was dusted for fingerprints. An elderly woman interviewed by an officer obtained the latest gory details of another murder in the City of Brotherly Love.

Peterson found Jackson first. "Is it Parker?"

"Yeah. Seems we got here a tad too late. Figures, don't it? I was unfortunately delayed gettin' here by havin' to deal with Parker's insurance company pals. Looks like Parker is definitely not the killer. Don't it?" Jackson gave a disgusted shrug. "A few minutes sooner, and we'd a caught the guy responsible. Damn!"

Hedley asked, "When did your boys get here?"

"Right before youse got here. We found him here on the floor."

Another officer, on his knees beside the body, looked up. "Say, sir? There's something sticking out between this guy's fingers. It's shiny. But I, uh can't get it … Oh, God! … loose. Jesus! Damn thing's stuck in there tight."

"It's called a death grip, Flannery." Jackson tapped the officer on the shoulder. "Let the forensics crew handle it. Ya ain't wearin' gloves. Yer contaminatin' the evidence."

"Oh, yeah, s-sorry," Flannery answered as he rose from the floor allowing the ME to take over.

Dominic Vitalli, knelt down beside Parker's corpse, and using long forceps, gently but firmly pulled at the metallic object. He was diligent as he tugged at what appeared to be a stickpin.

"This is what you're looking for, Trev? It's a gold pin. And, guess what? It's a match to the one in the Turner, Costello and Ramirez cases. It's an initial 'E'. There are some fibers attached to the closed end of it. When I get back to the lab, if I can identify the fibers, maybe we can finally get the culprit and solve this thing once and for all."

Jackson stared at the pin. "Doesn't fit. Who do we know with the initial, 'E', as their first name?"

Hedley offered, "I do. And, if it's who I suspect, someone I know is in big trouble. Gotta go, guys to take care of business. C'mon, Frank."

PINNED FOR DEATH

***

After Hedley and Peterson left the crime scene, police activity continued.

Vitally and Jackson exchanged troubled looks.

Jackson stated. "Parker gave us a clue to his murder. Maybe Costello has a partner. Do ya think?"

Vitally got up from the floor. "Well-l, maybe. Meanwhile, I need to bag this one up and ride with him to the morgue. I'm waiting for some DNA results dealing with the Regina Costello case."

"Ah, the murdered sister who was preggers. Yeah, you g'head, and report to me whatcha find out about *that* case. I'll need to stay here and help out."

"Okay. When I find out anything, I'll give you a call. See you."

"See ya, Dom," Jackson reached in his pocket and pulled out a small bottle of TUMS Extra Strength. He unscrewed the cap and shook out a handful and popped them into his mouth in one swift gesture. *God, this job is sure gettin' to my belly somethin' awful.*

Vitalli gave Jackson a sympathetic shake of his head, turned toward the body on the floor. "Okay, boys. Bag him, load him up, and I'll take care of things from my end. Let's go."

Jackson's thoughts disturbed him.

Where the hell is Marco Costello? Who's this other person? Just what we need, another complication.

Chapter 26

Vitalli arrived at the morgue with Richard Parker's body. Two assistants placed the bagged corpse on the examination table and unzipped the bag. Vitalli thanked them as they left. He removed the bag from around the body of the young man.

"Well, fella, you'll keep for a while. There's something I need to check out first, then I'll come back to you. Sit tight," he patted the body's left leg.

Vitalli wanted to see whether or not the DNA sample from Regina Costello's amniotic fluid came back. The coroner had his suspicions of who the father might be.

If I ask Trev to get DNA samples from the girl's father and her boyfriend, I could determine paternity.

Vitalli checked the inbox for the DNA report, but didn't find it. He knew he had the copy of the request in his files. He took it out of its folder and called Jessie Barton, the head lab tech, to see what the holdup was.

"I don't have any record of a DNA test from you dealing with the Costello case, baby," Jessie informed the ME. "When did you put the request in?"

"It was five days ago. Look, Jessie, I have a copy of it right here."

"I believe you, sugar, but it isn't here."

"You're sure."

Jessie insisted. "Damn sure, I'm sure. You know me by now. I don't let things get by me no way, no how."

"I know. If anyone around here is thorough, it's certainly you. It's just so strange."

"Well, I can't do anything without a sample. Give me a sample, and I'll do it for you ASAP. Okay?"

"Sure thing. I'll get on it straight away. And Jess?"

"Yes?"

"You may have cleared something up without even doing a thing. Thanks."

"For what?"

"For just being there."

"Okay," Jessie hung up puzzled.

Vitalli hung up. *So, Marco Costello, alias Bobby Pieri, your little diversion didn't do squat.*

Chapter 27

Alison needed to refresh herself before plunging into the research on the Costello case. She found the door to the ladies' room locked and knocked to find out if anyone was in there. When there wasn't any response, Alison called out and a soft, mumbled voice answered. She heard scrambling behind the closed door, and finally, when the lock clicked, it opened. Lakeesha stood in the doorway.

Alison noticed the bruises on her friend's face, as she entered the room. "Keesh! What the hell happened to you?"

She quickly pulled Alison into the room and closed the bathroom door. "My dad came home last night and ragged out on me about you and me last Wednesday night. He called me a drunken fool. Like he's not. Right?"

"Who told him about us going out together?"

Lakeesha sported a sheepish grin on her face. "Guess I did. He beat me and threw me outta the house." Then, beginning to sob, she continued, "He-he threatened to call the cops on me if I tried to get back home. I-I tried to get back in this morning, but he had already changed the locks. What am I gonna do? I got nowhere to go."

"My God. Where did you stay the night?"

"In my car," the poor girl answered.

"The whole night?"

"Yup. And it was freezing cold last night, but I was afraid to keep my car running. I didn't wanna get asphyxiated."

"The man's an utter idiot."

"That's my dad for you."

"Keesh, look, you're coming home with me. I'll give you my spare keys to Ramirez's house and my apartment there."

"No, no, no. I can't do it to you. I-I can't let my problems go where you live. You got enough on your plate with Richie Parker trying to come after you. Don't worry about me, I'll be fine. I can't do it." Lakeesha protested, very upset.

"Keesh, you're going to stay with me."

"No!" Lakeesha insisted, beginning to cry.

Alison wrapped Lakeesha in her arms. "Until your dad cools off. How about it? It's nothing permanent. Besides, with Ramirez being dead, I'd really like the company. Her house is so big, quiet and empty. Somebody's gotta come stay with me for a while to kinda fill it up. Whaddaya say? C'mon, Keesh. It's not forever. Just for a little while. You know, 'til you patch things up with your dad."

"Rent. Figure out a fair—"

Alison held the poor girl at arm's length. "Rent? To who? Ramirez's ghost? Oh, no. No-o way. You're in trouble with Dad, and you need a place to stay. You're staying as my guest. Not a bad deal, is it?"

"But, but— "

"Remember, girlfriend," Alison a little smile creased her face, "we're keeping our butts outta this."

Lakeesha returned the smile, but it hurt the left side of her face. She grimaced as she muttered a brief thanks.

"Fix yourself up, and I'll buy us some lunch." Alison gave Lakeesha a gentle hug.

Lakeesha sniffed back tears. "Ya know somethin', Allie?"

"What?"

"You're the best. I owe you, this time. I really do owe you."

"Keesh, you don't owe me a thing. Being my friend through all this is payment enough. Now, I'm springing, but you gotta choose."

"How about those wings we never ordered with some fries?"

"Why not? I'll call The Lunch Stop, and top it all off with two Oreo cookie milkshakes. Okay?"

"You bet."

"I'll be back before you know it."

Alison left to call in for lunch. Lakeesha Ellis looked back in the mirror at the nasty bruises on her face, which made her feel even more miserable. Cosmetics couldn't even conceal the deep purple-bluish blotches on her deep-brown complexion. She decided to keep her sunglasses on to fend off the sensitivity she felt when her eyes were exposed to the harsh fluorescent lights in the office.

Everybody probably knows what happened to me by how I look anyway.

Lakeesha walked out of the ladies' room and made her way back to her cubicle, trying to avoid the stares and whispers of her co-workers. When she returned to her workstation, she settled down into her seat to begin processing case files.

Within the hour Alison returned with the ordered food and stopped at Lakeesha's cubicle.

"Hey. How 'bout we eat right here? It's more private. Okay?"

"Sounds good to me," she shrugged her narrow shoulders.

Lakeesha removed the files she had been working on and let them flop on the floor. She found some paper towels and arranged them on her desk like a makeshift tablecloth. Alison removed the food from both bags she carried and placed the items on the towels. Lakeesha laid out some extra paper napkins she always stored in a drawer and shared them with Alison. They happily ate and chatted about the weekend to come.

When they were finished eating, Alison said, "Keesh, I hafta stay a bit later tonight, 'cause I'm really into the research on the Costello case. I'll try not to stay too long, so here are the extra keys. Now this one with the weird hole at the top opens the house, and this one with the red band on the top opens the apartment from either the connecting door, or the back steps. Okay?"

"Okay, thanks. And thanks for treating. The lunch tasted extra good today."

"My pleasure. See ya back at Ramirez's place."

"Okay. See ya, girlfriend."

***

The rest of the day was uneventful as Alison began putting the pieces together on the Costello case. She wrote a timeline of the events leading up to Costello's conviction and where people were in relation to Marco Costello. She made a copy for Humphrey and made a note to herself to drop the copy off to him before she left for the day. With everyone involved in the case in their proper place, Alison felt she was on to something.

What she discovered revealed Marco was at the insurance convention, and several of Marco's friends verified where he was at the time of Jeannette's murder. The signed registration paper stated he was there. But was Parker there? There wasn't anything proving Parker attended the convention at all. Unless he didn't sign in, and why didn't he, if he attended the convention? The fact proved what Alison told Ramirez. Parker killed Jeannette Turner. If Parker wasn't at the convention, then he had to be in Philadelphia. Because where else would he have been?

Chapter 28

Lakeesha Ellis cleared her desk when she noticed desk clock read 5:15 p.m. She didn't mean to stay after 5:00, but time simply got away from her. After logging off her computer, she locked her desk, and reached for her hat, coat and gloves. She checked her reflection in the mirror she kept behind her door. *S*he gingerly touched her bruised face. *Oh, Lawdy, Lawdy! The left side of my face turned real funky colors since lunch.* Lakeesha passed by Alison's desk and said goodnight to her.

"Remember, don't stay too late."

"I won't. See ya later, Keesh."

Lakeesha caught an elevator going down, as its doors were about to close.

***

Forty minutes later, Lakeesha parked her car in front of the Ramirez house. From the glare of the streetlight, she could see the two-story masonry home nestled among evergreens and shrubs on the front lawn. The cobbled walkway led to the front door, and she climbed the four steps to the entrance. With the key Alison had given her, she unlocked the door and entered. She wanted to take another look at the house the lawyer lived in and decided to take a quick tour to get an idea of the kind of home she wanted for herself some day. Lakeesha turned on the light by the front door, took off her gloves, stuffed them in her coat pockets and began unbuttoning her coat when she heard a noise she couldn't quite identify coming from the rear of the house. She stopped trying to hear the sound more clearly. She was startled, but thought Alison had come home earlier than expected.

She couldn't be home now. I just arrived myself.

"Allie? Are you here?"

The scuffling sound stopped.

"Hello?"

No answer.

Maybe it was just my imagination.

Not hearing anything else, Lakeesha took off her hat and coat and placed them on a chair opposite the front door.

Lakeesha didn't notice a shadowy figure stealthily approaching her from behind holding a candlestick above his head. She turned around at the last minute, and the phantom quickly placed the object on the floor behind him. Lakeesha, taken off guard, asked, "Who the hell are you? And what's on the floor?"

Ignoring her question, "Hi, Lakeesha."

Recognizing the voice she tore off his ski mask. "Huh? Marco? What the hell you doing here?"

"I'm not Marco. I'm Bobby."

"Like hell you are. You're Marco Costello. Alison showed me your picture. Why all the lying?

You're nothin' but a liar and a cheat. I thought we had something, you and me. But it was all a lie, wasn't it? This time I know Daddy was right about you. Shoulda listened."

Marco came close enough to stroke her cheek. "What happened to your face? Whatjadoo? Run into Daddy's fist again?"

Lakeesha smacked his hand away. "Get your dirty hands off me. My dad still can't get over our being together." Pointing to her bruises, she added. "This is your fault. Of all people to run into. And here of all places. Anyway how did you get in?"

Marco dangled his set of lock picks in front of her face. "With my handy little bag of tricks."

"That's unlawful entry, you dope. Why the hell are you here, anyway? Anyone else finds you here sneaking around, I'm implicated. So, if you have half a mind, get outta here. And stay the hell out."

"Not 'till I get what I came for," he answered.

"Huh? Like what?"

"It's something I need."

"Is it so important you want go to jail for breaking into this place? Listen, I'm trying to do you a favor. If you don't get outta here right now, I call the cops on you."

"Like hell, you will. Not with our history, babe."

"Just watch me." Lakeesha turned to grab the phone on the table by the door.

PINNED FOR DEATH

Marco struck her across the right temple with the candlestick he picked up from the floor beside him. Lakeesha fell in a heap. As she lay unconscious on the parquet floor, Marco went over to her and noticed she was still breathing. He picked up the dropped phone with a gloved hand and replaced it on the receiver. He hid the candlestick behind the chair in the living room.

Shit! Where's that Alison chick? I need to get the file. She must keep the file with her. I'll hafta come back later.

After turning out the light, Marco crept out of the house, peering from the front door trying to determine if anyone was outside. Positive no one was around, he left the Ramirez house. He closed the door. After he left, the door sprung open and remained ajar.

***

Around 7:00 p.m. Alison arrived at the Ramirez house. She hurried directly to the main house instead of her apartment because the front door was open wide.

Keesh wouldn't leave the door open. Something's up.

Frantic, Alison called out to her friend. When Lakeesha didn't answer, Alison really became alarmed. She turned the living room light on and found Lakeesha on the parquet floor, her head surrounded by a pool of blood.

"Omigod! Keesh. C'mon, Keesh. Answer me," she screamed, kneeling over her friend.

Not being able to rouse the girl, Alison punched in 9-1-1 on Ramirez's land line phone. She quickly reported the break-in and an ambulance. While Alison nervously waited for help to arrive, she kept checking on her friend's condition, which hadn't changed.

The ambulance arrived and two medics came to the front door carrying a gurney. They checked Lakeesha's vital signs. One of the medics placed a breathing mask over the young girl's nose and mouth and took her pulse. Both medics placed her on the gurney. The driver came out of the ambulance to take information from Alison, who became very agitated seeing her friend lying on the stretcher not responding to treatment.

Two minutes later, a squad car came, with its lights flashing. People began coming out of their homes wanting to know what the commotion was. The Ramirez home was cordoned off with yellow caution tape to prevent anyone corrupting the crime scene.

"Omigod! Omigod! What's wrong with her? I-I came home, found the front door open and her lying on the floor. I shoulda been here. I shoulda come home with Keesh, but stupid me had to stay late again. Damn, damn, double damn." Alison cried as one of the officers began taking notes of the incident. Alison gave the policeman Lakeesha's name and home address.

With Lakeesha secured to the gurney, the attendants loaded her into the vehicle. Alison insisted on going along. She accompanied her friend to the hospital. The ambulance made its way to Chestnut Hill Hospital.

***

Thomas Ellis arrived at the hospital. While the physician and staff nurses tended Lakeesha's wound, Alison waited outside the hospital room. From the corner of her eye, she spotted Ellis walking closer.

She ran up to the man. "Are you her father?"

Ellis answered, "Yes."

Alison yelled, "You almost had her killed. You bastard. Damn you! Why did you have to throw Keesh outta the house? Why? See what you did? Because of you she could've died from the maniac going after me. She's my best friend. And it's your fault she's here in that room." Alison raved and cried, while pounding on the man's chest with riveting blows.

"What the hell? Who the hell are you?" Ellis asked. "Stop! Stop this, right now. Somebody get this looney offa me. I need to be with my little girl. I wanna see my little baby." Ellis sobbed.

One of the attending nurses attempted to pull Alison away from the man, but the girl began swinging her fists at him, too. The nurse was able to fend off the blows when he managed to grab one of Alison's arms and pushed it back behind her.

Alison screamed at the top of her lungs full of rage, "Let me at him. Just let me at him. He's gonna pay for this. I'll see to it."

"Miss Caldwell. Calm down. Calm down, right now. This is not the time or the place to vent," the nurse soothed the girl and pulled her away from Ellis. Alison, finally calm, was ushered away. She went home dejected.

Ellis entered the hospital room.

"W-what's her condition? How did this happen? The police didn't tell me too much of nuthin'." Ellis shook from grief, as he saw his only daughter fighting for her life. She appeared so tiny in the hospital bed, almost shriveled.

"Mr. Ellis, I'm Dr. Luellen Canfield. Lakeesha suffered severe blunt force trauma from a blow to the right side of her head. She's breathing on her own, but the prognosis isn't good. I've placed her in a drug-induced coma until the swelling of her brain goes down. The next twenty-four hours are the most crucial and should tell us something. There's really nothing we can do for her now. We'll have to wait it out."

PINNED FOR DEATH

Ellis was dumbfounded and could say nothing. He sat alongside Lakeesha's bed and stared at her.

Chapter 29

Hedley and Peterson came to Alison's apartment behind Carlotta Ramirez's house. Anxious to get the job done, both officers raced up the stairs. When they reached the top of the outside staircase, Hedley rang the doorbell.

Hedley said to Peterson, "I don't know how she's going to take this."

"Well, look, Mick, ya gotta do what ya gotta do. I know ya like the girl, but this is official biz, and she ..." Peterson waved his fingers in the air.

With much apprehension, Alison came to the door and brushed the curtain aside to see who it was.

"Miss Caldwell?" Peterson asked through the curtained door.

"Y-yes?"

"It's Frank Peterson and Mick Hedley. Open up. We need to see you."

"Oh, yeah, thank God, thank God. Oh, yeah. Yeah. Oh, Mick. I-I mean Officer Hedley," Alison corrected herself when she brushed the curtain aside and recognized Hedley. She blushed. "Officer Peterson. I remember you from Weirded-out Wednesday two weeks ago. Please, please come in," she unlocked the apartment door.

"I'm so glad you're here. I've been so worried since Keesh was assaulted two nights ago. I'm glad you're here to protect me. I thought all this stuff was taken care of, when I like told the officer who took the info I gave her over the phone, I received two more threatening notes at work."

"We're here to … Wait a minute? Did you say you received two more threatening letters?" Peterson asked.

"Yeah. Isn't it why you're here?"

Peterson ignored Alison's question. "When did you get them?"

"Hm-m, one was last Monday, I think, and the other was, let's see … two days ago. One was left on my desk at work. Both letters had my name on them, so the mail clerk dropped them off on my desk. He knows me." Alison thought for a minute. "Right. Definitely two days ago, because I was researching another case I had been assigned."

Hedley asked, "And you brought both letters to the station?"

"Well, yeah. I didn't want 'em hanging around. I did open them because they came with the other mail I got at work."

"And you read them?" Hedley prompted.

"Yeah. After the third one came, I really got scared. The original one was bad enough, but to get two more. It's when I called the station to report them."

Hedley asked, "Are they from the same person?"

She answered while shrugging her narrow shoulders, "I-I guess so. Who else could they be from?"

"It's a shame we don't have those letters here so we could—"

"Wait, wait, wait. Yes I do. I made copies of them before turning then in," she said as she ran into her bedroom.

"Y-you what?" Hedley raised his eyebrows.

When Alison returned, she informed the officers, "I make copies of everything I think is important. So here they are."

"Real smart of you," Peterson said, very impressed. He scrutinized both letters. The content of the letters appeared similar to the original one Alison received. They stated she would be killed if she reported anything to the police.

"I'm really glad you came. But I didn't ask for the police to come. So you're here because—" Alison raised her eyebrows.

Peterson stated, "A restraining order has been issued against you. And we came by to inform you about it. We have the copy from the judge."

"A what?"

Hedley explained. "Alison, Thomas Ellis is pressing charges against you."

"For what? For saving his daughter's life the other night?"

"No, for assaulting him. You can't be closer than five hundred feet from him at any given time," Peterson recited from the document.

"Let me see that. I can't believe the asshole. A restraining order."

"Alison, Ellis can do whatever he wants to in an assault situation," Hedley stated.

Alison read the order. She went over to the sofa and sat down. Continuing to read, without looking up from the paper, "I see. What about hospital visits to see Keesh?"

Hedley said, "Only if Ellis isn't there."

Looking up, Alison smacked her hand down in anger on the coffee table, "I can't even visit my friend?"

"Not if he's there," Hedley looked over at her.

Getting up from the sofa, "Oh, Mick, c'mon. I did the man a favor, and this is how I'm rewarded? So I bruised his ego a little."

Peterson said, "From his statement, you bruised more than his ego. You punched him out."

"I didn't punch him out. He's lying. I went after him with my fists, I admit, but he stood straight and tall when I left the hospital. And so what? He deserved what I did to him. After all, Daddy Dearest threw her out of the house. And why? Because she and me had the nerve to become a little drunk one night. Do you realize she had to sleep all night in her car? Remember the last two weeks have been so damn cold at night, she could've had frostbite and lost some fingers or toes. So I took her in, with my good graces, and she nearly gets herself killed by some idiot who broke into this house. Do you know I visit her in the hospital after work to see how she's doing?"

"And how is she doing?" Hedley asked.

"No change. They stopped the meds to see if she can come out of the coma by herself, but she hasn't so far. They told me," Alison began to sob, "if she stays in the coma much longer, she could stay that way forever. Forever. Do you hear me? Forever! And the man, who calls himself her father, has the nerve to wanna put me in jail for saving Keesh's life. How fair is that? You should see her, she's so pretty laying in bed. She looks like an angel fast asleep, and I talk to her all the time I'm there by her bedside to try to make her wake up, but she doesn't, and—" Alison broke down and cried.

Hedley came over to her and placed his arm around her shoulders. Alison turned into his chest and cried quietly. When she finally stopped, she looked up into his gentle eyes. "What can I do? I feel so guilty. I hafta see her, I just have to. It's not fair for him to do this to me."

"No, Alison, it's not, but you need to play by the rules. If you violate the restraining order, you *could* be placed in jail," he answered.

Angered, she yelled, "What? Me? Go to jail?"

Peterson began to say something to Alison and glared at Hedley, but Hedley returned a stern look and Peterson kept quiet, while trying to soothe Alison.

"Can't the order be reversed, or something?" she sniffed back tears.

"Not unless Ellis is convinced you're no longer a threat to him," Hedley looked into her eyes.

She broke away from Hedley in anger. "Oh, God! Like what kind of a threat could I *be* to him? He's six-feet something-or-other, and I'm about five-feet three. What's he afraid of, I'll smack him in the knee? I don't think so."

Peterson offered. "We're here serving you with the order and a warning."

"What're you gonna do about Keesh? Is anybody investigating what happened here? I mean, she coulda been killed."

"We don't believe this was a bona fide break-in," Peterson stated.

"Why?"

"Because we really think the guy Lakeesha found in your house was after something he thought you or Carlotta Ramirez had in your possession and didn't find it. Nothing was taken. We're going to need your help in finding it," Hedley explained.

"But what could it be?" Alison sniffed away tears.

"Maybe it could have something to do with the Costello case," he suggested.

"How do you know?"

Realization caught up with her. "Ohhhhh, shit! The file. It *was* Parker. You're right. The guy wasn't here robbing the house, he was looking for the file. Parker probably thought Ramirez kept it or Lakeesha had it, and when he didn't find it, he tried to kill her."

"Where's this file?" Hedley asked.

"It's here in my apartment. I've been working very hard trying to piece things together on the Costello case. It's been taking up most of my time, and I brought it home. It's why I worked late when Keesh was attacked. Oh, God! What happened to her *is* my fault."

Hedley reached out to her. "Alison, don't blame yourself for what the perp did."

Peterson added. "We are gonna get you police protection. I'll make sure a patrol car watches the house."

"We need your cooperation to catch the guy who did this," Hedley put in.

"Cooperation? You'll get it. I swear."

"If the killer is on the loose, then it's only a matter of time—"

Alison's heart sank, "You think Parker'll come after me here, don't you, Mick, I-I mean Officer Hedley?"

She began pacing back and forth.

206

PINNED FOR DEATH

"Alison, what's going through your mind?" asked Hedley.

"Sh-h! Let me think for a minute. Just let me think this one out. The thought of being under police surveillance scares the shit outta me. Sorry! I don't mean to diss you, but I hear this all the time about witnesses who get caught up in police biz and get murdered for their trouble," Alison stopped pacing and faced both men. "But."

"But?" Both officers were puzzled.

"Yeah. I was put on this case to do one thing: Find out the truth about what really happened to Jeannette Turner and why Marco Costello had been framed. The only other person involved is Richard Parker. Right? Well, let's look at Parker. Did Richard Parker kill Jeannette and have Marco take the rap? Was it an accident? Or, was it planned? We don't know, do we?"

"No." Both men agreed in unison.

"Well, the only way we'll know for sure, is if I, Alison Caldwell, give you a little assistance. I'm willing to act as bait to help flush out Richard Parker and to make him admit to Jeannette's murder. Maybe I can find out why he set up Marco, and if he killed Regina Costello and why."

"Uh, the other reason why we're here is to—"

Alison interrupted Peterson. "Look, you don't mind me calling you Frank, do you?"

Peterson shook his head with a smile.

"I won't be any trouble. I can take of myself, and I promise to report anything … Uh, why are you two looking at me that way?"

Hedley came closer to her. "Alison, Frank and I appreciate your wanting to help, but there's something you don't know."

"What's that?"

"Frank and I went to have a little chat with Parker at his home the other day, and—"

"And?" Alison urged Hedley on, her eyebrows lifted.

Peterson answered for him, "Parker's dead."

"He's dead? No shit!"

"Yup!" Peterson replied.

Alison didn't say a word. She flopped back onto the sofa and held her head in her hands.

Hedley knelt next to her asking, "Alison, are you all right?"

Shaking her head, "Hell, no. God. Parker's dead. *Now* what?"

Peterson said, "We hafta find out who killed Parker."

"I know who it *wasn't*," Alison offered.

"Who is it?" Peterson wanted to know.

"Regina's fiancé is her father's partner in his business. So he couldn't be involved. Regina and him were gonna get married. She was pregnant, you know."

"Oh, yeah?" Peterson asked.

Alison nodded still holding her head with both hands.

"How do you know?" Peterson wanted to know.

"Her coat. When she came into our office earlier the day of her murder, she had on this beautiful, expensive coat, and it didn't fit right in the waist. It was too tight there. The only thing I could think of why it was so tight, was she was pregnant."

"So about this boyfriend," Peterson urged.

"Fiancé," Alison looked up and corrected Peterson.

"Okay, fiancé. What's his name?" Peterson continued the interview.

"Uh, didn't you check him out already?" Alison asked.

"Frank, don't you remember? Eddie Something-or-other, the guy who stopped by the morgue to collect the Costello woman's things."

Alison interrupted, "Wait a minute. Wouldn't Regina Costello's family want to do it? Isn't it a bit unusual for her family to let her guy collect the clothes and stuff?"

Hedley answered, "No, not really. Especially if they were living together. You mentioned she was pregnant. The guy probably did her family a favor."

"Well, I guess … What a yucky favor," Alison shuddered at the thought. "But, now, how do we get to the killer? Everybody else involved in this case winds up dead. Jeannette Turner, Regina Costello, Ramirez, and now Parker. The only one left is Marco. I really hoped for Regina and her family's sake she was right. Her brother didn't kill Jeannette. So I guess he did it after all," Alison sighed. "There's really nobody else but Marco."

"If Marco rifled through Carlotta's things," Peterson suggested, "we should go through with your plan, Alison, to flush him out."

Hedley warned. "You know how dangerous this is, don't you? You really want to put her in the soup?"

Alison insisted. "Yeah, Mick, but what other choice do we have? At least my idea is better than being carted off to jail for trying to do someone a favor and not being appreciated for it. And besides, now this case is really personal. I do have a stake in this because of Ramirez and now Keesh. She got hurt because she was in the wrong place at the wrong time. Ramirez was killed because she got too close to solving the Costello case. I know it. And I'd really feel guilty not being able to do something to solve this thing even though I really didn't like the bitch. Pardon my French," she rolled her eyes in exasperation. "But I sure didn't want Ramirez dead."

"Are you certain you want to do this, Alison?"

Alison looked into Hedley's eyes with conviction. "As sure as I'll ever be. I can do this." Staring at both men she insisted, "You guys will be protecting me, so I know I'll be safe. Consider this fate. If I hadn't turned the wrong way down Ramstead Street nobody would've discovered Regina's body for God knows how long. I saved you a step, didn't I?"

Peterson smiled. "Yeah, we certainly can't argue with you on that one." He added, "You saved us quite a few steps."

Hedley glared at Peterson. "Alison, how are you going to go about this? To trap Marco, I mean."

"Mick, I'll just do what I normally do. You know, continue to work on the case, make sure all the i's are dotted and the t's are crossed. I could wear a wire. I can start by asking questions around the insurance company Marco and Richard worked for. Make it obvious I've taken up the case. Oh, and oh. This is even sweeter. I can visit some of the fancy restaurants and flash around Regina's picture. Ask some of the patrons if they remember seeing her with someone other than her fiancé. A secret boyfriend, an acquaintance, or something. So if Marco gets close enough to me, you know, my asking questions about Jeannette and Regina, to some people, and really putting myself out there where he might be and my being very vulnerable, you guys can come in and get him. How's that sound?"

Before both officers could answer, she added, "And-and if I can make him admit what he did and he delivers, you got him on tape."

Hedley's blue eyes flashed harshly. "Absolutely not. You're putting yourself in real jeopardy with the scheme you're suggesting, and I won't have it." He warned. "No way are you to do any detecting. We are the law, understand?"

"But—"

Hedley pointed a finger at Alison. "But, nothing. You are a paralegal. Do your job and let us do ours. Okay?"

Resigned to the fact, she didn't get her way, Alison replied, "Okay."

Hedley asked, "What about relatives? Shouldn't you be thinking about living with your parents for awhile? To avoid all this?"

"Zip. My parents are perfectly content to live there in their mental island paradise. So it's a definite no."

"Meanwhile, we're going to put a patrol car on this street. Do you have your cell phone?"

"Yes, Mick, when I went to the Roundhouse, the receptionist gave it back to me."

"Good. And I want you to keep it on you at all times. Is your phone handy?"

"Yes, I'll get it for you," Alison excused herself from the room to get the phone from her purse.

Alison returned from her bedroom. "Since that awful Wednesday night, I've made sure it always has a good charge. Here it is."

PINNED FOR DEATH

"Thanks," Hedley took the phone from her and pushed some buttons. When he finished returned the phone to her. He explained, "All cells have a GPS chip inside. As long as the phone's on, we will know where you are. If you need to call us, punch the number two for speed dial, and we'll be right on the line."

"So, do you have a plan for me?"

Peterson explained. "Yes, go about your business. Go to work."

"How about me wearing a wire?"

Hedley emphasized, "No wire." More gently, he added, "You'll be protected because we're only a phone call away. Keep your cell charged to the max. The perp who sent you those letters might try to contact you. We can track him down and capture him before he tries any funny stuff." Hedley didn't want to alarm Alison with what crossed his mind.

Hedley stood. "Well, that's all for now. C'mon, Frank we have some investigating to do. Alison, you know what you're supposed to do. No detecting on your part, and you'll be safe."

"Okay. Whatever you guys say." *Only a phone call away? Thanks guys for the safety net.*

Chapter 30

Relieved she hadn't received any more threatening letters, Alison concentrate on her work load. She resumed her normal routine, which became only more hectic due to the turn of events involving the Costello case. She needed to report to Thomas Humphrey, which still gave her a lingering sense of guilt every time she stepped into his office. Although no one had been told of her indiscretion at the Back Draught, she still suffered bouts of either an upset or knotted stomach and felt much trepidation each time she entered his office.

Humphrey asked Alison to go to the City Morgue. When she returned to her workstation, Alison reviewed the copy of the autopsy report of Jeannette Turner's exhumed body the medical examiner gave her. The report showed Jeannette suffered a single fatal knife wound to the heart. Upon the medical examiner's further inspection, the dead woman's decomposed body showed no further evidence.

What she read about the autopsy report on Jeannette Turner and the Regina Costello case proved both women were killed under similar circumstances.

She decided to call Officer Mick Hedley about her suspicions.

Hedley answered on the first ring. "Miss Caldwell, are you all right?"

PINNED FOR DEATH

"Yes, oh, uh, everything's okay with me. I've been going over the Costello case, and I need to tell you what I've found. The only thing connecting the Turner and Costello murders was the way in which they were killed. The knife wound is making me think they were both murdered by the same person. Same wound. Same person. If it's true, then Marco definitely did kill Jeannette Turner. Jeeze, this seems to make Marco Costello a serial killer." She shuddered.

"Alison, you are getting way out of –"

She continued. "But why did he wait two years to kill Regina? From what I know about serial killers, they stake out their victims and kill them one after the other. They don't wait too long to make their next kill. I guess. Unless some serial killers *do* wait for their next victim. But in this case, the two-year wait doesn't make sense to me. After Regina died, Carlotta was killed next, then Parker. So why did Marco wait two years between Jeannette Turner and Regina Costello, but kill Carlotta Ramirez and Richard Parker right away? That's what's making me think Jeannette's murder was unplanned. It could've been an accident. But then, why all the other killings? This *really* doesn't make any sense. Whoever did the first two killings must have had all the time in the world. The thought of somebody waiting around to pick his next victim makes me really scared."

"Listen to me. I appreciate your wanting to help. The button on your cell should only be used in a strict emergency. Do you understand?"

"Yes, but—"

"But nothing. Interfering with police procedures will get you into trouble. Is that perfectly clear?"

"Yes."

Hedley insisted. "Okay, then. Since there's nothing else to discuss. We're done."

"Yep." *That's what you think.*

***

Peterson leaned against the doorframe to Hedley's office. "Hey, Mick, ya ready to go?"

Hedley scratched his chin. "Yeah. I guess so."

"It's the Caldwell girl, isn't it."

"You got it. I have a bad feeling she's gonna stick her nose into something she won't be able to get it out of."

"Look, you done all you can at this point. We're on speed dial on her phone. You warned her a dozen times. You put a watch on her street. What else can you do?"

Hedley didn't answer.

"Mick, what's goin' on in your mind? I see wheels turnin'."

"Alison brought up a point."

"What's that?"

"The fiancé. Marco hasn't been around, but nobody's seen Eddie Sandroni around either. The killer could be Marco, but it could be this Eddie person too."

"Whatcha gonna do about it?"

"Frank, let's just say. I'm thinking hard. Very hard."

"But what—"

"Leave it to me. I have friends in high places."

Peterson shrugged his shoulders. "Okay. C'mon now, let's detect what we gotta detect."

***

Hedley and Peterson retraced Regina Costello's route on the fateful Wednesday before the Thanksgiving holiday. After Regina left the offices of Dunbar Engels and Quinn, she was seen shopping at several downtown Philadelphia boutiques.

"We're Officers Michael Hedley and Francis Peterson, P.D. We're here on an investigation of a recent murder, and we need to ask you some questions."

Alarmed, the store clerk at Gentleman's Calling, an exclusive men's store on Chestnut Street, said around 5:00 p.m., he was especially concerned over a young woman fitting Regina Costello's description. "With my assistance, she purchased two men's outfits and the stuffed bag was quite cumbersome. I worried how the young woman would be able to manage the rest of her bags, because the others were overstuffed as well and I suspected the woman to be ill."

Hedley prompted. "What made you think she was ill?"

The store clerk continued. "Ms. Costello held her stomach, as if she attempted to hide feelings of what appeared to be nausea. Even though she told me of her needs, the young woman insisted she was fine. I still suspected something was wrong but didn't want to press the matter."

Hedley asked. "What else did you observe?"

"After the sale was rung up, I handed her the receipt along with her American Express credit card. She replaced in her purse as I handed over the bag of clothing to her. The name on the credit card was definitely Regina Costello's."

"Why do you remember her name?"

"It stuck out in my mind because she experienced difficulty with the other purchases made from other stores. I offered to hold the items she had charged until she finished with the day's affairs, but Ms. Costello refused saying she planned to leave the city right after a prearranged dinner engagement at La Mediterranean."

After Hedley scribbled in his notebook, he inquired, "What time did Ms. Costello leave your store?"

PINNED FOR DEATH

The store clerk thought for a moment then stated, "Ms. Costello left the store sometime around 5:45 p.m. heading toward 8th and Market Streets. She wanted to hail a taxi into order to go to the restaurant. I opened the door for her and noticed she didn't wait too long for a cab. Instead she walked the one block, I assume, to the El entrance on Market Street. I was very concerned for her welfare, so I watched her progress until she turned off Chestnut Street."

Peterson asked. "Is there anything else you remember?"

"Nothing I can recall."

Hedley stopped writing, closed his notebook and thanked the clerk.

***

The officers' next stop was the restaurant.

They learned from the maitre d' at La Mediterranean Regina Costello kept her dinner appointment with her father at the restaurant. She arrived at 6:30 p.m.

"Name, please," Hedley said.

"Uh, Pierre LeBoef," the maitre d' emphasized his French accent.

Hedley's eyes widened. "Pierre LeBoef? Peter Beef? Is it your real name, or just for the atmosphere of this place? You know it can always be checked out by payroll."

The man hesitated then finally answered the detective in a more realistic Philadelphian accent, "Okay. You're right. The name is really Peter Birenbaum. I use my stage name for ambience," he said with a flourish of both arms. The young man dressed in an extremely tight tuxedo, revealing not only a well-developed muscular figure but an obvious bulge in his pants staring at Hedley. The bright purple shirt caught Hedley's eye.

"Pierre LeBoef," Hedley muttered as he pulled out his notebook.

"Yeah, LeBoef. Like Shia LeBoef."

"Yeah, buddy. He's a bona fide actor. Not some phony—" Peterson interjected.

"Frank, let it go. Let it go. This is police business, so let's continue, okay?"

Peterson began to protest, but Hedley stopped him by giving his partner an angry look. Certain Peterson was quiet, Hedley continued the interview. Hedley prompted Birenbaum, "Give us a rundown of what happened on Wednesday night November 22nd, the night in question. We're investigating a murder."

Birenbaum asked, "Wait a minute. Murder investigation? What murder? When did you say?"

Hedley clarified, "We're investigating the murder of Regina Costello, who we understand, came to this restaurant the night she was killed. We need to ask you some questions."

PINNED FOR DEATH

Horrified, the man placed both hands on his face exclaimed, "Omigod! Oh, dear. Regina Costello dead?" Birenbaum uncovered his face. Deep in thought, he shifted his weight on one foot, put one hand on a hip, scratched his goatee with the other and looked at Hedley. "Let me see ... Yes, I do remember ... Wednesday evening. Well, Ms. Costello came in for dinner with her father. From where I stood, I could see things progressed without incident until, towards the end of the meal, the young woman began acting very agitated. Ms. Costello began shouting at this point, rose from her seat at the table and abruptly left. She either forgot or deliberately left her purchases behind. After Ms. Costello left the restaurant, I discreetly glanced over to the table and noticed her father called someone on his cell phone."

Peterson asked, "And who do you think it was?"

Hedley looked at his partner in disbelief. Birnbaum rolled his eyes while drawing one hand to his chest, "Like I would really know. I have no idea. Like I said, I discreetly noticed his pulling out his cell phone to call someone. Mr. Costello stayed until he finished the last of his wine."

"Discreetly." Hedley repeated.

"Yes, discreetly. But, I do remember something else."

"What was it?"

"Well, Mr. Costello received a call some time later."

"How much later?"

"Look, I really couldn't pay too much attention. The restaurant filled with patrons, and my attention was entirely on assisting them. I'm just telling what I noticed and approximately when things were happening. When Mr. Costello finished his second call, the call he received, he appeared to be angry with whomever he spoke to and raised his voice."

"Were you able to hear what he said to the person?"

"No, officer. His table was at the far side of the dining room, and I needed to stay at my station here up front. What I did notice, however, Mr. Costello became quite agitated as he raised his voice into the instrument. His voice was louder, but I couldn't make out what he said. The restaurant filled almost to capacity by then, and the background noise drowned out his voice."

Hedley looked up after writing more notes. "Do you think the phone conversation he had with the person had any relation to Ms. Costello's leaving the restaurant?"

"It's a possibility."

"What makes you think so?"

"Because Mr. Costello made the call immediately after she left."

PINNED FOR DEATH

"What did Costello do after he received the other phone call?"

"Well, he stayed until he finished another glass of wine. I noticed something else about him, too."

Hedley urged. "What was it?"

Birenbaum explained. "Well, you see, uh, I thought it very strange what he did after he hung up. He finished his glass of wine, and held it up as if looking *into* the glass like he studied it. Then, he banged the glass down on the table very angrily. The way he did it made me think he was going to break the crystal. He sat at the table for a few minutes. Then abruptly stood, gathered the packages from the seat next to him. He took out five C-notes, placed them on the table and left."

"How did you know the denominations of the bills?"

"You should've heard the raves of the server as he passed me on his way to the kitchen after clearing the table."

"I see. Is there anything else you'd like to add?"

"Officer, I see all kinds of crazy things going on in this place. And this is one helluva a posh restaurant here. Mr. Costello acted *determined* to do something. Like something happened he needed to fix right away, you know?"

"Why do you think Costello acted that way?"

"Hell if I know." Then sudden realization hit Birenbaum as he placed a hand up near his throat and exclaimed, "Omigod! Do you think he had a contract put out on his daughter? How could he live with himself?"

Hedley answered, "Why do you say a contract?"

Birenbaum put a finger up near his mouth then whispered, "Because he's Italian, you know. The name. Costello. Hello?"

Peterson interjected, "Just because the man's Italian don't mean he's a Mafioso. Jesus God."

"That's enough, Frank." To Birenbaum, Hedley said, "Thanks for your help. We'll continue with our investigation. You're not thinking of leaving town, anytime soon, are you?"

"No, why?"

"In case we need to come back and talk to you again. It's just routine."

The man gulped, saying, "I'll be here. Working."

"Okay. Well, thanks again for your help."

Hedley closed his notebook and both officers left the restaurant.

When they were out onto the street, Peterson placed his hands on his hips. "Thanks for your help? What was that all about? Didn't Mr. Homo shake up the Italian side of your family tree?"

"No way. Are you telling me you're Mr. Homo-phobic?" Hedley winked.

"Not me." Peterson laughed, shook his head and threw both hands up in the air. The officers walked back to the patrol car.

Chirp. Chirp.

Hedley picked up the car phone.

"Officer Hedley here … Yes. We'll take the call. We're on our way." He hung up the instrument.

Curious, Peterson asked, "What's up?"

"Uh, oh. Looks like we're going to pull another all nighter. It's a double homicide in Society Hill this time. Let's go."

Chapter 31

Alison returned to the apartment behind Carlotta's house exhausted from her day and hoped to relax. The work load had piled up all week. The tension from seeing Thomas Humphrey, at the office also took its toll.

At night, she suffered nightmares about the video she took of him dancing in a wildly spinning fury at the Back Draught. The horrid dreams always ended with his face practically mashed against hers with an accusatory finger pointed at her, bellowing, "You're fired, Miss Caldwell!" while her co-workers' large distorted faces stared at her in an unforgiving manner. Before she could defend herself, she always awoke in a sweat.

The past few nights she had deliberately delayed going to sleep, but tonight she planned to go to bed around nine despite the nasty dreams. Tiredness consumed her as she made her way to the bedroom. She clicked off the light from the small lamp resting on the nightstand by her bed, and fell asleep quickly.

***

A dark figure parked his car on the street opposite the Ramirez home. He could see the neighborhood was quiet. No one around. Determined, he made certain he had the needed tools, left the car and crossed the street.

***

After hearing unmistakable loud rumblings, Alison woke up. At first, uncertain whether or not she still dreamed, when fully awake, she realized what she heard was definitely not her imagination. The sounds were real. Terribly real. Alison got out of bed and rushed toward the connecting door. She placed her ear to it trying to determine exactly what the noises were, and if, in fact, there was an intruder. She couldn't. It seemed as though the disruption came from everywhere and nowhere specific. She froze when she heard an unusually loud sound coming from downstairs.

THUMP. THUMP. THUMP!

What the hell? Did something fall over? No, it's the killer! Alison broke into a sweat. "This is one time I wish Carlotta were here. If you're up there listening please lend a hand, a wing, a halo, whatever you got. I need you real bad. I thought I was in deep shit before, but nothing compares to this."

She went to the coat closet and took out her overcoat. Instinct told her to grab the Marco Costello file and hide it in the zip-out lining. Alison turned her head and looked over at the window.

Experiencing an adrenaline rush, she reached into the outside pouch of her purse and found the cell.

With a shaking finger, she punched the number two immediately connecting to Mike Hedley's office phone. Alison was sweating profusely as she heard ring after ring of the instrument. *Damn! He's not picking up. He said I could call him 24/7, but he's not there. I'll leave a message.* "Officer Mick, it's Alison Caldwell. I'm in trouble. Come to the apartment quick."

Alison made certain her cell had a full charge and dropped it into the inside pocket of her overcoat. She zipped it closed. She put on the coat, slipped on a pair of shoes and walked over to the window and raised it. "I don't believe I'm gonna do this. But it's the only way out."

Terrified she took a deep breath to steady her nerves, bent down and climbed out onto the roof closing the window carefully behind her. Alison walked toward the front of the house. She took a brief scan of the street from her perch on the roof and saw nothing. Not a squad car in sight.

Thanks, police guys. Thanks for being my protectors. Either they're so well hidden, I can't see them; or they're not around. Don't look down. Look straight ahead and go for it.

Maintaining her balance, Alison held both arms out and crept along the steeply slanted cold roof. With slow and deliberate steps, she made her way across. Compensation for the roof's deep angle took its toll on her slim legs. Alison needed to hike up her coat; its length impeded her progress. Her left calf began to ache, because she needed to keep it tightly bent. The trellis, lining the outer edge of the roof, was a few yards ahead of her. Due to the intense cold night, her feet were becoming numb. She ignored her discomfort and moved on.

Just a little bit more.

Alison almost tripped over some kid's baseball. She kicked it away and watched it bounce down to street level. She stopped to catch her breath and turned her head to look down to the street wondering if anyone watched her. She saw no one and heard nothing.

She grabbed for the railing a few steps ahead. Alison thought it would be sturdy enough to hold her weight. To her dismay, it was loose. Alison's slender body made the sway with her weight. She almost put her foot down wrong on a loose shingle.

That was close. Don't need a bum ankle to complicate my life. The trellis isn't so far. It's so close. A bit more.

"Oh, God, Carlotta help me, please, please, please. Forget whatever I said about you before. I really didn't mean all those dumb things. Let me get to the trellis, I'll be good. I'll be good, I swear. Be my angel, pleeeese."

A few feet more and she made it.

Oh, yes! There definitely is a God. Thank you, St. Carlotta of the Loose Railing, thank you, thank you. Alison hugged the trellis for dear life. After almost slipping off the trellis midway, she caught herself in time and she calmly climbed down to street level. Alison squeezed her eyes shut, not believing she made it in one piece.

I'm safe, I'm safe, I'm safe. It's so good to be on solid ground ...

Opening her eyes, "Oh, fuck." Alison looked through the trellis into eyes staring back at her.

Chapter 32

The intruder came around from behind the trellis. The dim light concealed his face. "Alison Caldwell? I need your help. Maybe you have what I'm looking for."

"W-who are you? And how do you know my name?"

The man grinned a crooked smile making Alison's heart stop. Her stomach took a nasty turn. "Never mind. I-I know exactly who you are. Y-you're Marco Costello."

He hesitated, then confessed. "Yeah. It's me. I'm in trouble."

Alison attempted to run, but Marco grabbed her arm which stopped her in her tracks.

"L-let go of me. Help! Help me! Somebody!"

He pulled her back and clamped a free hand over Alison's mouth. She managed to bite down on a finger. "Ow! Dammit!" His grip on her relaxed as he rubbed the injured digit. "Look what you did. You almost bit my finger off."

"Shame it wasn't something else." Next, she saw her chance and kicked him in the crotch.

He bent over in pain. "And you got one hell of a … right … leg. Damn! The Eagles could sure use you as their star kicker. I'm not gonna hurt you. I swear."

"I don't believe you. Why are you here and why in hell do you think I'd help *you*?"

Marco could barely straighten up. "Because you're my only chance. I need you to help me outta the mess I'm in. Please, please, you gotta help me. I don't know what else to do or where to turn."

A little braver, Alison offered. "How about going to the police?"

"The police? Are you kidding me? I'd be back in jail before you know it."

"Which is where you should be. How did you know where I lived?"

"Oh, I didn't know where *you* lived. I knew where Carlotta Ramirez lived from this … a copy of the receipt she signed when she went to the morgue," he pulled out a piece of paper from a pocket. "Here, look."

She squinted reading Ramirez' name in the feeble light. "The morgue. Oh yeah, you work at the morgue."

"Yeah, I do."

"It's why you know so much medical stuff."

She had another realization. "Was it *you* in the street that night? Are you the guy I saw the night of your sister's body?"

Ignoring her question, Marco's eyes widened. "You found Regina?"

PINNED FOR DEATH

"Yeah, I did and almost tripped over her, thank you very much. How could you kill your sister?"

"I didn't. Could we go inside and talk?"

"Are you kidding me? No way."

"Please, Alison. I promise I won't bite."

Alison pursed her lips. *Now where have I heard that before?*

"C'mon. I've been framed, and you're my only hope."

"There are a whole string of bodies proving otherwise."

Alison looked at him. Deep in her soul she knew he shouldn't be trusted. She decided to give it one last effort. The girl sprinted into the darkness. Marco caught up to her, spun her around, then punched her in the face. Alison walked a few steps, turned and gave him a puzzled look, then crumpled into his arms.

Chapter 33

"Uh," Alison groaned. Barely able to open her eyes, the room's chandelier's light stabbed at them making her squint. Her head ached so badly as if she relived her nasty hangover from the Wednesday night with Lakeesha.

"Sorry, Alison. You okay?"

Alison mumbled a "Whatever." She moaned, still woozy from the blow to her face. The room took a vicious spin when she attempted to raise her head from the couch. She laid her head back on a cushion.

"Oh God. Where am I?" Alison slowly raised herself from the couch while looking around the room. "Oh, never mind. I know exactly where I am."

"Do you feel better? I could get you some water."

She glared at him. "No, thanks, Marco. I'll be fine."

"You gotta trust me."

"Yeah, right. Really. Let's see. I should trust you after scaring the shit outta me, accosting me in the middle of the night, almost pulling my arm out of its socket, and punching me out. Gee, does that sound trustworthy to you?"

"Will you help me?"

"Where's my cell?"

"It's in your coat pocket."

"Get it. Now. I'm calling the police again."

PINNED FOR DEATH

Marco protested. "Don't call. I can't—"

Alison's voice boomed. "Get the damn phone. Remember the kick I gave you outside? I'll give you one worse in here." She held out a hand.

Marco did as asked. Alison made the 9-1-1 call giving the dispatcher the information.

"While we're waiting you're gonna tell me everything from the time Jeannette was killed to the present. Spill."

"Aren't you afraid I'll kill you?"

Alison smirked. "You could've done me in at any time. So I think I'm safe at least for the moment." She frowned and crossed her arms over her chest. "Talk."

"I had a terrible falling out with Dad about Jeannette. He wanted me, no, he insisted I break things off with her."

"Why? Wasn't she Italian enough for him?"

Marco sighed. "Far from it. She was passing."

"Passing? Passing what? Drugs?"

"Hell, no. Passing for white. Jeannette was black and Dad didn't want a *la femmina nera*, as he put it, messin' up the family stock."

Alison sniffed and thought about Jeannette's photograph in the Costello file. The dead girl's striking features especially the haunting dark blue eyes.

"Daddy's a real piece of work. So how did Jeannette wind up dead?"

"I don't know. I called her up to wait for me at my apartment because I didn't want to stay at the insurance convention for the whole day. When I got home, I found her on the floor with a knife stickin' in her chest."

"What did you do then?"

"I called my buddy from work, Richie Parker to help me clean things up."

"Wasn't he at the convention, too?"

"We left together."

"From what I know about you two, you guys spend a lot of time together."

"Huh?"

Alison sniffed. "Never mind. Why didn't you call 9-1-1 and report her death?"

He sat on the couch and placed both hands on his head. "I don't know. I was scared and thought the police would think I did it. Richie came over, and we decided to, take care of the body."

"Oh, by making things difficult for identification. Am I right? And how did you get Richie to agree to do this for you?"

"Well, we played the ponies. Wentworth Insurance is a prestigious company. If anyone found out about any shady dealings by employees, they would be terminated."

"So, in a way, Richie was your insurance. Pun intended. Whose idea was it to put Jeannette in the dumpster?"

Marco hesitated. "Uh—"

"C'mon. *I* won't bite. Promise."

"We both thought it was a good idea at the time, and no one would find her. No one did until some street guy found her scrounging for food."

"How did you know about this street guy?"

"Read it in the papers."

Alison shook her head in disgust. "So, how did Regina wind up dead?"

"I really don't know. I saw her and—"

Alison's brows arched. "Wait just a damn minute. She knew you were out and about?"

Marco continued. "Well, she didn't know I was out 'til she saw me that night. Dad knew 'cause he bribed a guard to look the other way so I could escape."

"Then where did you stay while you were 'out'?"

"At Richie's place."

"Did you have any contact with your parents?"

"Only with Dad."

"Richie and I had it with Philly, so we agreed to leave the city. There wasn't anything for us here anymore. I couldn't face my family. Jeannette was dead, Regina was dead. So we're planning to go tomorrow morning. Richie bought the plane tickets."

Alison studied Marco's face. *He doesn't know Richie Parker's dead. Didn't mention Ramirez either.*

Unless Marco is a bona fide psycho, he doesn't know they're dead.

"Marco, I believe you."

"Why?"

"I just do. Whose babies were they?"

He didn't answer.

Alison shook him. "I asked you whose babies was Regina carrying?"

Marco looked up at Alison. "Richie's. She met with Dad to tell him she was breaking the engagement with Eddie Sandroni. She must've told him about the pregnancy and her and Richie 'cause Dad was really pissed off when he called me and spoke to me. He wanted me to catch up with her to make Regina listen to reason, but she wouldn't. She pushed me away and stormed off into the night. I tried to follow her, but she got lost in the crowd. It was the last time I saw her. Next time I saw her she was—" He looked down at the floor. "I-I saw her body laid out in the morgue."

She almost had sympathy for Marco. "Since you were posing as Bobby Pieri, you couldn't reveal who she was to anyone. Am I right?"

"Yeah. I couldn't draw attention to myself. Under the circumstances, I … Alison, I can't go back to jail. I can't do it. I'm innocent of murder."

"Maybe, maybe not. But you're definitely guilty of everything else." She tapped her chin with an index finger. "Let's rack up the charges. You

238

exchanged IDs with another person, escaped from jail, broke into Ramirez's house, assaulted my bestie and put her in the hospital, and scared the shit outta me. How'm I doing, Marco? By the time you *are* released from prison, if ever, you'll be using a walker."

Chapter 34

The rookie cop, Ian Feeley, motioned to Detective
Trevor Jackson. "Sir."

"Yeah, Feeley?"

"Just got a call from Hedley. He and Peterson
were tied up with two homicides. Hedley's worried
about a Caldwell girl who sent him a distress call
earlier. Do you know anything about it?"

"Damn. I know everything about it. Have
dispatch check on the Caldwell girl's GPS."

"You got it," Feeley punched numbers on his
cell. Dispatch answered informing the young cop the
GPS from Alison's cell gave a weak signal of her
whereabouts.

"Have you been able to pinpoint where she
is?" Jackson pressed Feeley.

"Yeah. The map I have shows she's at the
Ramirez house."

"He got 'er. He got 'er, dammit. How long
will it take us to get there? Been a while since she
called Hedley?" Jackson bent over and peered at the
computer's screen.

"Yes, sir. The time? About fifteen minutes
ago. Her position isn't moving. Guess we can get to
her in about twenty-five or thirty."

Detective Jackson barked. "Not good enough.
Get a hold of dispatch and tell 'em to get a SWAT
team out there ASAP. We'll meet 'em there. She

could be trapped by the perp. For all we know Alison's in major deep shit by now. Get a move on, will ya? Never mind. Gimme your cell." The detective grabbed Feeley's phone and yelled orders into the instrument. "Dispatch. Get the SWAT team and squad cars out at the Ramirez house. Send them out to the location on the double. There's a victim trapped by a killer. Cordon off the area around the intersection. Get medics out there, too. Move it now."

If it were possible, Jackson would have kicked himself in the ass. *Where's the patrol car guarding the Caldwell girl?*

Detective Jackson ran out with Feeley and the squad of men. He opened the passenger side of Feeley's car and sat in the seat but forgot to fasten the seatbelt. Instead, he reached for the bottle of Extra Strength TUMS in his pocket, opened it and chomped down several straight from the container.

"Feeley," Jackson said through a mouthful of antacid. "Move it. Get to the Ramirez house yesterday. C'mon, c'mon! Floor this thing."

"Y-yes, sir." Feeley stomped on the accelerator causing Jackson to be almost catapulted to the back seat. The detective muttered a curse and strapped on his seat belt. The squad car screeched its way out of police headquarters' parking lot and sped into the night.

Feeley turned so fast onto Race Street the car fish-tailed barely missing a woman crossing the intersection at 13th Street.

"Watch out! Dammit. You almost made road kill out of that woman."

"S-sorry, sir." The cop stammered, looking over at Jackson.

"And keep your eyes on the road. Dammit. Don't make *us* road kill."

"I-I'm doing the best I can, sir." Feeley focused his eyes on the road ahead.

On through the night they sped on Race Street heading west to the ramp leading to the Vine Street expressway. The patrol car fled a few miles to the Schuylkill Expressway, then shot off the Chestnut Hill exit. The squad car nearly spun off the ramp. At the last moment, the rear tires caught and the car leaped ahead as if it were a bullet shot from a gun. Jackson gripped the handhold so hard with his right hand his knuckles whitened. He glared at Feeley who offered a goofy grin in apology.

When they arrived at the Ramirez residence, they met up with three other patrol cars. The SWAT team was there too. The van, parked at an odd angle in the middle of the intersection, prevented any other vehicles entering.

Some lights turned on from several homes on the block. Only the very curious stepped out into the night trying to determine what happened. Officers from other police vehicles shooed them away from the possible crime scene.

Both men got out of the squad car. Feeley asked Jackson, "How do we handle this, sir?"

"Very carefully. The SWAT team is in control. Let 'em do their job. So step aside."

Feeley obeyed. Cautiously and with guns held in front of them, Jackson and Feeley scanned the street for any signs of movement. They saw most of the house encased in darkness except for a bright light coming from one of the downstairs rooms.

The SWAT team approached the home. On the commander's cue, one hit with a battering ram broke in the front door.

Jackson and Feeley followed the SWAT team and found a scared Alison Caldwell standing in front of a man. The team entered with their weapons at the ready.

The detective ordered. "Let her go and nobody gets hurt."

"Y-you can't take me back to jail. You can't."

"Buddy, it'll be better for ya if ya do as I say."

Alison turned her head, looked at her captor and stammered, "Y-you better do as he says."

Jackson asked, "Who're you?"

The man stood silent.

Alison answered, "H-he's, Marco Costello. In the flesh."

"Marco Costello? The guy in the coma?"

"He's the guy you're after. He escaped from prison. Marco broke into the house. I-I—"

Marco blurted out. "This is all a mistake. A terrible mistake. It's not what it looks like. I didn't kill anybody. I swear."

Jackson said, "Be cool and let Alison go. It'll be easier for ya. Trust me."

"I *did* trust the police and my damn lawyer. And where did it get me? In jail. I'm not going back. No way." Marco stepped backward dragging Alison with him. "I have something here that'll explain everything." He released his grip on the girl, looked down at his pocket and pulled something out.

A shot came from somewhere behind Jackson. Marco fell to the ground.

Alison gasped.

Jackson ordered, "Feeley. Check 'im, will ya?"

"Yes, sir. I'm right on it." Feeley bent down beside Costello and checked for a pulse. The rookie shook his head and looked up at Jackson.

Wide eyed, Alison exclaimed. "How could you? He was gonna to show you what he had in his pocket. You killed him." She raised her hands to her face. "You didn't have to do that. He was scared is all." She broke down in uncontrollable sobs. "Marco wanted to show you a pair of tickets. He didn't kill Richie Parker and he wouldn't't've killed me."

"You really don't know that. Marco could've told you anything to save his own skin."

"But … but—"

"Alison, it's over. The killer's dead. Let's get you to the hospital to check you out. Give your statement there. You're safe now." Jackson covered her with his overcoat.

"Thanks," she buried her head into Jackson and sobbed in relief. After a short time, Alison looked up into Jackson's face and sniffed back tears.

"C'mon, now. Let's get ya outta here."

Alison shuddered. *Somehow I don't think it* is *over.*

Chapter 35

A few nights later

A dark figure approached the Ramirez home and was startled by a distinctive scratching sound. The noise was only a field mouse. The intruder paid no further attention to it. Surveying the property found nothing else. The skeleton key from a key ring held in a gloved hand unlocked the front door. There was utter darkness. Quietness pervaded throughout the Ramirez house.

"Good. Rest easy 'til I get you, Alison Caldwell."

A cursory inspection of the downstairs revealed no one around. The intruder climbed the staircase careful not to disturb the sleeping young woman in the apartment behind the connecting door. At first there was difficulty unlocking the door. Scraping and jiggling the skeleton key into the lock along with a final forced turn, the door opened at last.

***

A sound startled Alison while getting ready for bed.

Oh, shit. Not again.

Curious, Alison listened intently, left the bedroom and focused on the noise. When she padded into the living room, she froze at the opened door.

PINNED FOR DEATH

"Oh, no! Who the hell are you?" Alison shouted.

The masked person announced. "I'm a special friend. I've come to be with you tonight." The intruder entered the room.

"Wh-what are you doing here? Wh-why—"

"What am I doing here? I'm here to see you, of course. There is some unfinished business needing attention."

"W-what unfinished business? I never saw you before, and I—"

"It doesn't matter whether or not you know me. What's more important is I know *you*. I know all about you. Who you are. Where you work. Your ties with the police. I've kept a good track on you."

Backing away, the girl felt nauseous. "It was *you*. You were out on Ramstead Street that terrible Wednesday night. You tried to get me to come with you to who knows where, and you wrote me those threatening letters, wasn't it?"

"No, it wasn't me."

"Bullshit." The young girl made an attempt to run to the bedroom. Her pursuer caught up and pulled Alison's long hair dragging her back.

"Ow! Lemme go."

The killer hissed in Alison's ear. "Forget it. You're the loose end that keeps getting in my way. We're leaving." The phantom kept tugging a screaming and scrambling Alison back toward the front door. She grabbed a table lamp and threw its shade aside.

The intruder kept pulling the poor girl. "Think you're smart? Do you? Think a lamp is going save you? You're a little insignificant bug." The intruder's laughter in diabolical cackles rang in the girl's ears.

Alison swung the lamp with menace gaining momentum. "Laugh all you want."

"Do you really think you can hurt me with your poor excuse for a weapon?"

Alison kicked backward hitting him in the shin. Her captor released the hold on her hair.

Alison feigned a move to the intruder's head, and instead she swung the lamp down toward a leg and hit square in the kneecap. The leg buckled as Alison heard a cry from agonizing pain.

"What's a matter? Having a bit of a problem? Are you hurt? How does it feel to be on the bad side of a lamp?"

"You broke my knee. You bitch."

"I'm glad." Alison waved the lamp in the air ready to strike again. "This'll make it permanent."

"You won't kill me."

"Wanna make a bet? You'd lose. You'd lose big time." Alison inched closer to her pursuer. She grabbed the black hood covering the face and yanked it off.

"Huh?" she exclaimed. "Who the hell are you?"

PINNED FOR DEATH

Through gritted teeth, the man introduced himself. "It won't matter if you know anyway. I'm Eddie Sandroni."

"Regina's fiancé? I don't believe it." The lamp dropped from her hand with a thud.

Despite agonizing pain, Sandroni saw his chance and made an attempt to retrieve it by crawling across the floor. "You'll believe it when I kill you."

Alison quickly stomped on the man's hand and ground it in. "Don't think so with a broken knee and a crushed hand."

The tortured man howled. "Get the fuck off me, damn you!"

Alison leered down at him. "No way. Now, tell me why you became a ruthless killer."

Breathing heavily, Sandroni stared up at Alison and confessed. "Yes. I did away with them all. Jeannette Turner was an abomination. She refused to leave Marco alone. So my business partner, Joseph Costello, asked me to do away with the problem, as he called her. I agreed because the old man was supposed to compensate me."

"Compensate you? How?"

"I'm getting to it."

"You mean to tell me Papa Costello told you to kill Jeannette? But Marco got pinned for her murder. He could've got the needle for something he didn't do."

"Well, Marco did get out, thanks to his dad."

Alison stared at the man in disbelief. "Continue."

"And, Regina. She betrayed me. We were supposed to get married. She was promised to me. Instead she had an affair with a disgusting lout of a man. Sneaking around with that-that Richard Parker. I took care of him by smashing his head in. Regina became pregnant with the idiot's kids. And, as for your lawyer friend, I followed her from work and whacked her because she put everything together. She got too close and found out what I had done. She would've told you before too long. And, as for *you*." Sandroni stopped massaging his injured knee. He pointed an accusing finger at Alison. "You had a hand in spoiling my plans to escape by picking, picking away at all the incriminating details. Even now you're standing in the way of my being completely safe."

"What's with the initial stickpins?"

Sandroni gave Alison a menacing sneer. "I was marking them. They were all pinned for death."

Alison stood with hands on hips in front of him and shoved his hand aside with her foot. "You mentioned you were going to be compensated for killing Jeannette. Were you paid for doing her?"

"I didn't get a penny for my trouble. Nothing."

"Then you must've been pretty pissed about it."

PINNED FOR DEATH

Sandroni fumed. "Yes. I don't like being disappointed."

Alison urged. "And?"

"Let's just say the Costello's are history."

"Mister and Missus?"

Sandroni looked up at Alison with a menacing smile. "Nobody gets the better of me. Nobody."

"What happened to the engagement ring?"

"I yanked it off Regina's finger and put it in my pocket. Hocked the damned thing for cash," Sandroni admitted.

"You're one piece of work," Alison picked up the lamp. She was ready to beat the man to death, and almost did when she heard footsteps bounding up the stairs.

She turned toward the door to the apartment and looked at the intruders. Alison breathed, "It's the police. How did you guys know to come here?"

One of the officers stated. "We've been watching this house for the past several days. A plain-clothes man spotted what was happening here tonight and alerted us at the station."

Next, Hedley burst into the room and saw the lamp raised above Alison's head, shouted, "Alison! You don't want to do anything stupid and have it on your conscience for the rest of your life."

Half sobbing, half screaming, she said, "Y-yes. Yes, I do. I want to kill him real bad for what he tried to do. For scaring the crap outta me. I've been

251

through enough. I want idiots like him not to mess
with me. Ever. Dammit."

Hedley called out to her, "Allie." Getting no
response, more forcefully, "Alison!" Hedley rushed
toward her. "Put the lamp down." More calmly, "Put
it down. We're here now, and we can take care of
things the right way."

Shocked into reality, she reluctantly complied,
sobbing, "Okay, okay. J-just get him out of here."

"H-how did you know to come to the rescue?"
Eddie Sandroni looked up, while being Mirandaized
and cuffed.

Hedley explained. "Two little things you
never counted on. One, the tickets to LA Richie
Parker bought for Marco and him." Hedley walked
over to Sandroni, pulling on the killer's lapel. "And
number two, what's really nailing you is this. When
you gave Parker the death blow, he managed to yank
off *your* initial pin. The initial, 'E', marks you as the
murderer. We wired this place a few days ago and
have your admission of guilt to Alison on tape. The
pin we found in Parker's hand ties you to the
murders."

Sandroni's eyes seethed with hate.

Alison Caldwell wept. Hedley grabbed her
and held her in his arms as she cried into his sleeve.
Ignoring Eddie Sandroni's protests and groans from
his injuries, Officer Frank Peterson pulled the

criminal up from the floor. "I'll need a hand here to get 'im into the wagon."

"This time, Allie, it's really over. It's all over," Hedley cradled her head in his arms. "Come with us to the station to make your statement."

"W-will you be t-there with me?" Alison sniffed back tears.

"Of course. I'll be with you always, Allie. Let's get your coat. C'mon I'll help you put it on. I'll take you to the station. Tomorrow, we'll go to the hospital to see your friend."

"What about the restraining order?"

Hedley sighed. "Papa Ellis isn't a problem anymore."

Alison looked up in Hedley's eyes. "Huh?"

"Trust me, he isn't."

Chapter 36

Six weeks later

Alison sat in the cushioned recliner provided by the helpful hospital staff. She sighed and looked at her friend. She placed the bookmark at the beginning of the next chapter, closed the book, rose from the chair, came closer to the bedside and gave Lakeesha Ellis a gentle kiss on her cheek.

"I'll be back tomorrow to continue Harry Potter's adventure."

Before she left the hospital room, Alison noticed something different as she looked upon her friend lying in the bed. The girl's hand definitely had moved. The fingers of Lakeesha's right hand were outstretched, not in their perpetual fist, and Alison thought her friend's hand attempted to reach out to her.

"Progress. I never stopped hoping, Keesh. I always knew there was a chance for you, and you made me see it."

Alison squeezed her friend's hand gently in answer. She left the room to tell the head nurse at the nurse's station.

PINNED FOR DEATH

He noticed Alison leaving the hospital. His halting, stumbling steps followed her at a safe distance careful not to lose sight of the young girl.

Alison. You didn't listen to me. I'm coming after you. I'll catch up to you soon.

ABOUT THE AUTHOR

Beverly Ann Meyers has been writing short stories for over twenty years. One story, in particular, *A Scent of Jasmine*, has been published online by *Bewildering Stories*.

She is the author of the supernatural novel, *Go to the Wish Monger* and is currently writing another murder mystery.

Beverly has attended several writers' conferences and is a member of The Wannabees, a professional writers' group.

A former middle school teacher, originally from Philadelphia, PA, she presently resides with her husband, Martin, and her cat, Callie, in Florida.

98145215R00146

Made in the USA
Columbia, SC
21 June 2018